Shadows in the Corners

1922

Ladies of Bottlebrush Grove Series

Olwyn Harris

The grasslands of the wilderness overflow;
the hills are clothed with gladness.
The meadows are covered with flocks
and the valleys are mantled with grain;
they shout for joy and sing.

(Psalm 64:12,13)

1

Published by: Reading Stones Publishing
Helen Brown & Wendy Wood
Woodwendy1982.wixsite.com/readingstones
Cover Design: Olwyn Harris -Some of the cover elements were created using AI technology.

For more copies contact the publisher at:

Glenburnie
212 Glenburnie Road
ROB ROY NSW 2360
Mobile: 0422 577 663
Email: Readingstonespublishing@gmail.com

Dedication:

For Shannon, who understands the shadows in the corners of life...

The joy is coming.

I

"Really Daddy, don't you think it is a little unreasonable that this is being scheduled right around Race Week?" Joy's plans were being thwarted, and although it was not often that she objected to anything, she could not be silent about this. This was a major plug in what she had been plotting in her head since last year's 'Race Week'. They sat together on the sweeping verandah, sipping from their cups in the white cane furniture that was placed so this aspect of the garden could be fully appreciated. She looked out over the manicured garden... 'parkland' would be a more accurate description. Wide lawns spread out like a deep green ocean studded with islands of flower beds and ornamental shrubs. Tree trunks swayed like the masts of tall-ships pitching in time with the tide. Joy sighed again.

Her father adjusted his rimmed spectacles and barely looked up from his newspaper. "Unfortunately, I am at the mercy of my contractors' availability. But when you think about it, Race Week makes perfect sense. It will be the best time to get it all sorted. You and your mother will be out and about, socialising as you do... and so, in my mind, this is an opportunity to make the disruption more manageable... *less* unreasonable."

"But..."

Mr Bramford folded his newspaper, took off his reading glasses and put them on the table beside him. "Come My Girl... Joy of my heart... how can we improve the future without disrupting the present? At some point we need to tolerate a level of inconvenience to be able to attend to these renovations that your mother has been waiting for so long to see completed."

Joy sighed once more and stared out at the mast-trees and wished she could sail away. She had never considered the virtue of patience to be her mother's domain. More accurately, Mrs Florence Bramford was infamously known for *not* waiting. Right now, Joy's own impatience was hardly willing to stay in check. "I know Daddy. I am disappointed, that's all."

Her father leant over and gave her hand a squeeze. "Chin up. You won't miss out on the racing season just because we are renovating here. You do love the races."

"Is that what you think? Huh." She really thought her father had more insight regarding her feelings about this. It was called a "week", but in actual fact, it was a much longer series of events with prescribed attention to hats, cocktail parties, music, sore feet, and boring conversation. Joy had been investing a lot of thinking time, planning and plotting, to find a way to escape this year's society-drenched Racing Season.

"Of course. You love the horses, and your mother loves hobnobbing with the fashionable folk."

"But Daddy, in truth I have been plotting all year a way to avoid all that. This project of yours has firmly put a stick in the spoke of my bicycle-wheels." Hole in her boat; pin in her balloon; derailed her train. All of the above.

"Correction. This is not *my* project... this venture is entirely your mother's," he said seriously.

Joy sighed again and poured them each another cup of tea from the cosy covered pot that sat beside the folded newspaper. "Regardless, what I am saying is that now you have scheduled this, I won't be able to defect from the season's events like I intended. Mother will not even allow me to stay home, cloistered away in my studio, if the place is overrun with contractors."

"Ahh. Now I understand. That makes more sense." He smiled and took another sip of tea. His daughter was so much like him in nature. More than anyone ever gave credit for. Perhaps it was her light hair and startling green eyes like her mother's, that threw them off. "Well, there is always a solution. Just make another plan."

"But Daddy..." The truth was that Joy could not see any other plan. She had put all her eggs in this basket, and she was bitterly disappointed. Her father was much older than her mother. He had been mistaken for Joy's grandfather on more than one occasion. Still, he had been Joy's ally all her life. She sipped her tea and tried again. "Actually, I have acquired a very significant commission, and it is so pressing that it cannot be put off..."

"You have a commission? What sort of client is so important that it cannot be put off for Race Week?"

Joy stalled. "Prestigious. Anonymous. Lucrative. They are paying well."

Her father's eyes danced in amusement. He chuckled and took another sip. "Sounds vaguely important. I wonder... how would I verify that you even have this so-called contract?"

She blinked her lashes slowly and pursed her lips. "Well... possibly... I could... show you the canvas..." She blinked and then sighed. Nothing got past her father. "Okay, I was going to try painting anyway. I've had little inclination for my art for such a long time, that I am determined to get back into it, even without a commission. This is a very good time to try. Just for fun. Last year Mother's entire agenda was to match me to some fashionable beau. I vowed that I was not going to put myself through that whole debacle again. And despite her strict criteria of eligible, those I am introduced to are all hideous, with their smooth talk, their two-toned shoes, top-hats, and bowties."

"And you seriously think that a fictitious art commission would be sufficient to divert your mother's match-making agenda this season? My Joy... I rarely suggest this, but I *don't* think you have thought this through."

"Oh, but I *have* thought it through Daddy. Over and over."

"Not adequately it would seem. A painting... even commissioned by the Governor General himself, will not get you out of Race Week. I'm sure of it."

"It won't?" She sighed. Of course, he was right.

"You need a reason with more... urgency. It will need to satisfy a complication in a matter that your mother is fully invested in. A commission for anyone, however important your client may be, will not be sufficient."

Joy looked at her father's eyes shining with all the mischief of a ten-year-old, planning truancy with a box of his uncle's cigars. "I believe you have an idea," she said curiously.

"Perhaps." He took another sip of his tea and leant back contentedly, gazing out over the lawns.

"Well then, tell me," said Joy impatiently. "Don't dangle a carrot like that and then say nothing more. Whatever it is, I am in."

He picked up a biscuit and sat back quietly for a while as he took a bite. "You know, I notice I am feeling quite tired. It is entirely possible that I am coming down with something, and I might, very soon, start to feel unwell." Joy's forehead creased in a frown, but before she could start to fuss, her father held up his hand firmly. "What this inexplicable fatigue means, is that I may need some help supervising the renovations. In fact, if you could front and manage the entire project, that would be very supportive of your father's pending incapacity." He lifted his teacup victoriously. "Voila! No Race Week."

She shook her head sceptically. "*Your* plan is to throw me into the deep end of a public swimming pool, and expect me to swim? How do you suppose that total immersion in the renovation will work? You know Mother would veto contact with workmen."

"Well normally, yes. But this is not a normal situation. We need to make sure that the contractors adequately attend to all the details that your mother has in mind. Besides, what your mother requires regarding plaster features and paint colours – all of those trappings, you will have more idea about those matters than I ever would."

"What you say does not make sense. You've managed all of Mother's projects! You know what she requires better than anyone." Joy stared at him, and then burst out laughing. "Oh! I get it! This is your *own* escape plan! You don't want to do Race Week either."

He raised his teacup like making a toast and sipped his tea. "Never have. And I don't intend to start this year. Besides, your mother's renovations are far too important. They have priority. They have urgency. They must be completed on time for her end of season party."

Joy quickly retraced her family history in her mind, like flicking the pages in a diary under her thumbs. She gasped. "Daddy! Not once. I have no memory of you ever coming to Race Week! And yet I have never noticed! How could I have not noticed something so monumental? You are the master of this ruse. I need to be your apprentice! Absolutely! I do. I need this."

"Oh, you are not so unskilled. See, even here you have been plotting detours with clear thinking, ingenuity, and determination. You have already realised the need to find a way to accommodate your preference without being rude, or antisocial, or ignorant."

"But yet, as you so accurately identified, I would not have been able to pull it off. You *are* the master," she said with a laugh.

"I must warn you My Joy, there is a serious side to all this plotting. I have rules. Never tell lies... only the truth. And for every escape, there is always a price. The cost of evading crowds of simpering socialites for weeks on end is that I must be content for one evening to attend your mother's party. Going to the End-of-Race-Week Party means I don't just turn up, but I must make the effort to join in, admire and be present. It is a ritual that I privately consider to be a celebration of effectively avoiding all the nonsense of the entire season."

"I can manage that," Joy said soberly. And like kids behind the school yard weather-shed, sealing a pact of intrigue with blood and spit, Joy poured another cup of tea, and settled in to conspire.

* * *

2

"But Mother... I have bought a new hat and shoes to go with my outfit, especially suitable to mark the beginning of the season. Then there are the other ensembles I found. I was looking forward to wearing them." No lie there. These were very nice outfits.

Florence Bramford scanned her daughter's purchases sympathetically. "Oh, Joy Dear, these are so stylish. Don't you think it is ironic that you have been so inclined to get in the festive feel of the season this year, and then this comes up to spoil it? I know how disappointing this must be. And I wouldn't ask, except you know that as Chair of the Ladies Guild I could not conceivably even risk *not* attending every one of the season's events. What if I got sick with your father's ailment? That would be an entirely impossible predicament! Your father is not up to doing this by himself. I'm sure you can appreciate the seriousness of the situation, given how quickly he has become unwell. It is very inconvenient that Bennet has been urgently called away on family matters at this time as well, otherwise he could have stepped up. Doctor Bertrand assures me that your father's affliction is not the Spanish Flu, but he feels it would be appropriate to isolate just to be sure." Doctor Bertrand was a familiar friend, and he was the only authority Mrs Bramford would listen to, regarding anything medical. Florence barely paused before she continued. "Your father assures me that if you were here, you could field questions, supervise details, especially when it comes to the décor. I don't need anything random happening that will clash with what we have already done. Just run things by your father if you have any doubts. He really needs your support."

"But Mother, you have already made all your selections on the colours, trims and architraves. We talked about each one."

"Of course... and the light fittings, fixtures and fabrics. Yes, it's all attended to. See, there is hardly anything left to do, but it is important that you are here to make a call if there are questions... so there are not hold-ups. We can't afford that."

"I don't suppose you would consider postponing. You have waited so long for these renovations on the loungeroom, what would another couple of months matter?"

"Postpone? Oh no, that is not an option! If we don't take advantages of this window, we could not conceivably start booking another contractor until February."

"Mother, if you are sure..." Joy allowed her mother to see her struggle with the proposed obligation. "Well then... I suppose. If you truly think there is no other way... then of course I must help where I can. That will be enough for my new outfit."

"Wonderful! Now go tell your father you are on board. It will relieve his mind. And don't forget to wear a mask. I think this is quite an adequate solution given the complexity of the dilemma."

Joy nodded her assent and tried not to look too eager. "I appreciate your confidence in my ability to handle this mother. I'm not sure I feel so fearless though."

"You will be fine. There is no other way."

"Then this is my mission: to ensure your end of season party goes smoothly as planned."

"Of course, Joy Dear. Be reassured, I have confirmed a number of eligible young men... Jacobs, and Gilmore and Mrs Van Alstyne's nephew... have all been invited to the party, so you won't miss being introduced. Not ideal of course, since others will have all the Race Week events to become acquainted. Still, it will have to suffice."

Huh. Joy turned away. *That* list was a sure-fire way to ruin a perfectly good subterfuge. "Well, I had better tell father that everything is proceeding as planned." Joy hoped that the way she said it conveyed her disappointment adequately. As she made her way out to the solarium that was being used as her father's sick room during the day, she restrained the light skip in her step and the smile on her lips, until she closed the door and was out of her mother's line of sight.

*   *   *

Joy watched her mother select another hatbox to add to the pile of luggage by her bedroom door. "I don't know why you are going to stay with Mrs Lincoln now – Race Week is still weeks away. It is unreasonable that you will be away with all the chaos that is about to break out here. Even with your planning it would be easier if you were here in the evenings so you could check in regarding the progress of the work."

Florence raised her hand and interrupted her daughter. "You underestimate how all-consuming planning these events are. It will be easier to attend to my committee responsibilities from there. I can't possibly risk being out of action if it happens that this sickness is something more serious. Just like Dr Bertrand said – just to be sure. Now remember, all the contractors must be out of the way by the last Thursday so we can set up for the party."

"Yes Mother. I will see to it: the work will be completed on time."

"Not just on time, it must be flawless."

Florence nodded as she folded another pair of gloves and placed them in the second suitcase open on her bed. She calculated something in her head and retrieved her travel jewellery box, checked its contents and then wrapped it in a scarf, added it to the other suitcase. The stack by the door was growing significantly. "Absolutely no delays. It can't be said often enough. Finding another suitable venue at this late hour would be quite impossible. And then you will be the Belle of the Ball," she said as if she had successfully constructed the perfect consolation prize, and nothing else needed to be said.

"I'm not sure how I will manage this to your satisfaction Mother."

"Have more confidence, Joy dear. We haven't raised you to be a wilting violet. With your father unwell... and not a word to anyone about this by the way... you know I have told Bertram most emphatically, that I will not have any white scarf hung on our door! That would simply mean we will be blacklisted for the whole season... not just our party. No, I am going to build the anticipation of the seasonal events undistracted by all the work here. There is so much to be done, I have enlisted Mrs Lincoln and Louisa to help. They are both delighted to have me join them."

"Louisa will be terribly disappointed I'm not going with you," said Joy with a sigh. Already she was weary of all the pretending.

"No doubt," Florence said unsympathetically as she snapped her suitcase shut with a flourish and paused as her husband appeared at the door. "James, darling, if only you were well enough to come with me. But Joy is here to look after you.

Mr Bramford raised his brow above his facemask. He moved aside as Dotty came and start juggling the numerous suitcases down the stairway. "My Dear... I promise I will not feel deserted. You are right. You should absolutely prioritise your seasonal responsibilities with the least amount of antagonism."

"It is disturbing that this bout of ill-health has hit you so hard. You are usually so robust. Has Dr Bertrand said anything further?"

"Just the oldest prescription of all My Dear: Rest." Mr Bramford turned away and coughed and sniffed. "Going with you would indeed be diverting..." He paused thoughtfully. "But I understand my civic duty to be socially responsible while I am convalescing. The air in your solarium is quite invigorating. The plants there are like a healing oasis. I'm sure the progress I am making is due to your foresight to have the greenhouse installed."

Florence paused at the door and squeezed her husband's hand affectionately. "Oh, you are such an old-fashioned grouch when you are unwell. Focus on getting better, and I will sort what is needed for Race Week at the Lincoln's. We do make such a fabulous team."

He chuckled and smiled. "Not a truer word was spoken Florence. Go. Attend your committee meetings. Work hard. But don't forget to relax as well. And I will recover while Joy sorts out these renovations so that the place is perfectly arranged for your little soiree at the end of all the festival fun."

Florence picked up her handbag and marched down the stairs. "I was thinking that we will hire extra hands from the caterers, to attend to the set up. There is such a lot to do, and we won't have our usual lead time."

Mr Bramford and Joy followed her down the stairs. "Sounds perfectly reasonable My Dear. This is why your Party is not just the highlight of Race Week but featured on the annual social calendar and always gets the most glamorous reviews." He barely restrained a yawn.

"Oh James, you are so very tired. Please, rest as Dr Bertrand has prescribed. I need you better for the party. Why don't you lie down, and I will have Joy bring you your breakfast tray."

"I promise I will be on top of my game by the party, My Dear."

"Of course. You never let me down, my darling. Not once. I live a perfectly fortunate life."

"You and me both, My Dear."

With that, Mrs Florence Bramford rushed out the door to vacate to her good friend Eliza Lincoln's estate. Joy watched her flee and then took her father's arm as they wandered together into the dining room to have breakfast. She said nothing while she ate her toast, amazed and relieved that their plan was actually working. This year she would finally escape the social chaos and have the space to paint over the weeks to come.

* * *

3

Mr Bramford reclined on his daybed reading his newspaper in the Solarium. This rather extensive greenhouse had been his wife's first quirky project. Her creativity had blossomed under his encouragement. The lush foliage, the fine water spray misting the exotic plants created a cool, verdant, shaded oasis, with an expensive array of ornate windows all around. Over the years, it became Mr Bramford's mainstay place to retreat and savour calm. Even though Mrs Bramford barely came here herself, he always referred to it as "her solarium", an acknowledgement that she had designed this wonderful space. The plants and flowers flourished under the combined attention of Mr Bramford, their House-Steward, Bennet, and their gardener's green thumb. Bennet made sure there were always freshly cut flowers in the main house. That was the only lingering matter Mrs Bramford seemed to care about when it came to the Solarium. Every so often she'd mentioned they had saved a fortune on flower arrangements, because of her thrifty initiative.

A pot of morning tea was sitting on the trolly beside him, snuggled in a tea-cosy, steaming from its spout. Mr Bramford looked up over his eyeglasses and saw Joy coming in with a notebook.

"So, do you share your mother's confidence that you are going to save the Race Week Party given the inconvenience of my being indisposed?"

She blinked and shrugged. "Apparently, I am adequately equipped to supervise the renovations while you recuperate."

"Are you sure you are okay with this? This is not exactly in the league of a commission for the Governor General."

"Well, I think you are right, Daddy – a decree from King George himself would not have been sufficient to escape the crowds. It won't be so bad. Mr Lincoln has put his best builder on the job, so a morning check-in will more than adequately address what is required. After that, I will have plenty of time to get back to my painting. This will be my personal artist's retreat. I am resolved to have an eagle-eyed focus."

Mr Bramford cleared his throat awkwardly. "Hmm. Well. I may have misjudged some of that. It may not be so simple. Unfortunately."

"What do you mean? Mother's plans are all set, and she insisted that Mr Lincoln send the Wilkinson crew. He did her last couple of jobs, so he is very familiar with Mother's expectations."

"He did. However, this letter came to say that Wilkinson has had a family crisis which has taken him out of town. Lincoln has subcontracted another guy with his own crew. He is coming today for a site inspection and preliminary meeting."

"Today?"

"Yes. But you should know his crew hasn't been together for that long. This was the only way that Lincoln could ensure we would meet the time frames. Wilkinson did give him a glowing reference though." He pulled a letter from the middle of his newspaper and handed it to her. "Not as experienced... obviously, given his age, but he assures me that this man does quality work."

She scanned the correspondence quickly. "Oh Daddy! No one uses a word like 'exemplary' unless they really think there's a problem."

Her father smiled disarmingly. "Joy Beatrice Bramford... you are leaking the cynicism of the very types you are going great lengths to avoid."

"Well apparently Mother's efforts to polish me up to look like her friends is almost complete."

"Good grief! Joy, I would expect you to follow your own course."

"Daddy – you sound exactly like Mother. Do you stand in front of each other and practice these lines?" She helped herself to a biscuit and poured herself a cup of tea with a frown.

"I have always encouraged you to be your own person. Do you know and love who you are? Do you really like her?"

Joy stared at her father in shock. She had not expected such a serious question, at least not this morning. She was still celebrating escaping Race Week crowds. "That was deep..." she murmured.

"Ahh. I am a fussy old coot – and an introvert. It is hard to be solitary if the company you keep is repulsive to you. God has been more patient and gracious with me on this quest to like my own company more than any other."

Joy sat on a stool beside her father and poured herself a cup of tea. After a pause she put down her cup. "Daddy, why did you marry Mother?"

"You know why."

"What I mean is... you don't seem to value the things she is fanatical about and you openly admit that you avoid just about everything that she likes."

"She enjoys what she does. It is important to her. I love watching her spread her wings... I saw it first when she was creating this solarium, and she did a wonderful job I might add."

"You know what I mean. How could you have possibly thought you would ever have anything in common?"

He shrugged and quietly drank his tea. "I was a widower... with a lot of money and no children. I needed a life change. And then your mother appeared... like a genie out of a bottle... sparkling and bejewelled with a vivaciousness for life that was totally intoxicating. The gossip rags called her a gold-digger, and me a blind fool. A fool maybe... but not blind. I was bored and I knew that life with your mother would never be dull. And then she bestowed on me the greatest gift of all. You. My Girl. Joy of my heart. Nothing she could ever do after you were born could be so terrible, because being your father has brought me nothing but joy."

"Oh Daddy... that is completely sweet of you. But how do you stay amiable in the face of all her social clambering? It annoys me so much. How you do it is a mystery to me."

"Not so mysterious. Like I said, I own my choices. I make them with my eyes wide, and my heart full. I like who I am. And I have no need to apologise that my wife likes different things. It may be old age... or it may be that I am just too tired to care for opinions anymore. I see a lot of people pass through my life who are rotten with discontent, and yet they mock the cost of pursuing contentment. I've done the other. I've been hungry with that insatiable appetite for ambition. But that kind of drivenness never made me content. You taught me a lot about contentment."

"Me? What could I possibly teach you?"

"When you were little... and out of sorts, or restless, or just tired... you would crawl up into my lap and lay your head on my chest. It didn't matter whether I was wearing on a fashionable dinner suit or plain gardening overalls. It didn't matter if I sat in an upholstered chair, or just an old bench in the garden. You would lay your head on my chest and then your breathing would slowly adjust to mine. Slowly, so slowly, we would synchronise. And then you would pull at my sleeves, or my lapels, or my collar... and giggle about some little joke that you could never explain. In an otherwise unremarkable childhood, when knees were scraped, and wills were challenged, that was the perfect picture of contentment for me."

"I know I could never be content with Race Week. That is why we are here."

"I was determined to befriend my own inner child, who has been hiding in the shadowy corners of my life. Every morning as I read my Bible, that is the time when I am most like that child who needs a safe place and be content. So, I clammer into the lap of my Heavenly Father, and stay there until I feel my breathing synchronise. It sets me up for the day. I do that when life is grim. Or when it glorious and profound. I stay there until I can find the joke that has been there all along, but I didn't have the eyes or the patience to see it before."

Joy frowned. "Daddy, are you sure this is just a ruse? Are you feeling quite well? You are more contemplative than usual. Is there nothing I can get for you?"

"No need to fuss," he said with a grin, "we have already established that I feel quite poorly. Now that your mother has clocked off for Race Week, let's go over her plans again. She is most concerned that the cohesive flow from the existing areas into the new not be compromised. You know the time frame is going to be very tight, right down to the finish line. The idea of Race Week, may have just taken on a new meaning." And he grinned, as if he had found the punchline to a particularly funny joke.

* * *

4

"Thank you, Dotty. Tell... umm... Galloway, did you say? Tell Mr Galloway that I will have my father to meet him on the verandah. Please bring us a tea-tray there."

Dotty offered a curt nod. "Yes Miss," and she left to assemble the required refreshments.

Joy quickly went into the Solarium and perched on the end of the daybed. Her father was in the depths of a biography. "Daddy," she whispered urgently, "the new subcontractor is here. You need to come and talk with him about the work."

Mr Bramford barely looked up from his book and quietly turned a page. "Don't forget I am in isolation. It wouldn't be appropriate for me to take a meeting at the moment, given the dubious nature of my health."

"But..."

"Does he look dull? I met the man a few times before Wilkinson palmed the job off to him. He seemed bright enough. I'm sure he will get the meaning of what is required."

"Daddy... please..." urged Joy. "He's a carpenter. I don't want to be taken as stupid, by ignorant tradesmen who disregard a women's ability."

"Then make sure you don't," was his only reply. He turned another page.

Joy found herself watching the rise and fall of her father's vest as he read. She waited until her breathing levelled and her anxious thoughts quietened.

He looked up. "My Joy, you know you cannot avoid this. It is part of the plan."

"I know Daddy. You've reminded me." She winked. "I was actually synchronising my breathing," she said as she stood to her feet. She had found that glimmer of fun in her eye again. "I'm sure he will try and dismiss me, but he may find that not as easy as he supposes." Yes, she was going to be all over this.

"That's My Girl." And he sat up and poured himself another cup of tea, that was no doubt as cold as stone.

She smiled at her own private joke. It amused her no end that her father had managed to use his story to his own advantage once more. He would not be moved from his books beside his daybed in the Solarium, with his facemask close by, in case Dotty's casual observations would cast doubt on the sincerity of his ailments. But Joy didn't mind. Race Week was her mother's annual escape, one that she anticipated and worked towards all year. Joy had always been obliged to go along with her on that 'holiday'. This time she was allowed to accompany her father on his vacation, and his style was more to her liking.

She cleared her throat and picked up the roll of plans from the sideboard as she left. This had a familiar feel about it. As a child, whenever Joy's shyness got the better of her, and she had urged her father to rescue her from something uncomfortable, he would firmly say, "Joy, you don't need a knight in shining armour. We can fight the monsters lurking in the corners together until you are confident enough to manage it yourself. You know, I believe you can do this." This was the same sage advice for piano recitals, tea parties, book reviews, and painting problems. She knew her father well enough; he had stepped back and would not be moved to intervene on her behalf unless everything fell apart and became a total mess. The humiliation of that idea, and the energy required to retrieve it back from the edge of catastrophe, meant her only course was to ensure that this never became a mess in the first place. That also meant that this new builder must never know that she was just her mother's mouthpiece. No, to give her voice credibility... this sub-contractor must believe that this project was her own project from beginning to end, and she was the driver of all these initiatives herself.

There was determination in her step as she walked out of the room, holding the plans. She wiped her palms down her drop-wasted day dress, and the rolls of plans she juggled under her arm fell clumsily to the floor. She hurriedly picked them up, took a breath, bracing her posture with her chin tilted, opened the French-doors and walked around the verandah to the table setting. The clack of her hard heels went silent as she stopped and looked at the man who was leaning on the rail in a relaxed slouch, gazing out over the garden.

He didn't turn, but quietly stated, "Sir, thank you for giving me this opportunity. The windows you've chosen will take full advantage of your beautiful garden. I agree with your wife, Mr Bramford: such a view of the garden should not be wasted."

Joy jolted and curiously looked at the back of his head. "You've looked over the plans then?"

He straightened up as she spoke, and turned, removing his felt hat in a singular, smooth movement. "Of course... Wilkinson passed them on." He pushed down his opinion that the project was excessive to say the least. Why make their generous lounge room even larger, in league of a ballroom? After all – this excess was now his bread and butter. He paused as he turned and laid eyes on the woman in front of him, her arms full of rolls of building plans and design layouts. Wilkinson had told him the mistress of the house was young... a 'looker' who had married for money, but even with the heads-up, he was surprised. This woman was much younger than the most vicious scandalmongers had led him to believe. He restrained a curl on his lip. It was an affront to solid, honest decency, that this woman would prostitute her pretty face for mercenary gain. "I apologise Ma'am, your housekeeper told me Mr Bramford would be meeting me. I was expecting him," he said rubbing his thumbs under his braces. "I understood he was old-fashioned like that."

"Sometimes what you expect is nothing like reality. Mr Bramford is actually very progressive in his support of my mo... my projects. Anyway, Mr Bramford is unwell and laid up. I will be your point of contact for this job." She put the rolls of plans on the table. "I trust you fully understand that it is imperative that this is all completed by the final Thursday of Race Week. We host a party on the Saturday that cannot be put off."

"If I start when you scheduled with Wilkinson, there will barely be sufficient time for what you want done. I don't have access to the men he has in his crew. And on top of that, given we are going into Race Week your timeframe is ridiculously optimistic. You have not planned this well, and I cannot be penalised for your lack of consideration."

She considered him quietly. "Well, you certainly are opinionated Mr Galloway. Actually, this renovation has been impeccably planned. I trust you have your crew and tradesmen sorted and on point. It is expected that you factored this into your acceptance of the job."

"I did, but mostly I took the job as a favour to Wilkinson. He understood those limitations when I agreed to take the job. Your time frame allows no margin. Predictably there will be delays that cannot be anticipated."

She stared at him patiently, like a tutor who was trying to teach a child to read time. "Can you do this or not?

He took a breath. "My meaning is that it is not *un*usual for even the best laid plans to be interrupted in some way. These hold-ups are outside my control. If you do not get your renovations completed in time for your function, I repeat, I cannot be penalised for these unforeseen delays if you have not allowed any margins."

"It seems to me, Mr Galloway, that you are declaring defeat before you have started. Wouldn't you have a work-around for such interruptions if you say they are so familiar?"

"Ma'am! My point is that the best work-around is to allow more margin. I cannot plan for what is unforeseen and unknown." How many ways could he say the same thing?

"Well, start earlier. Start today if that will provide you the margin you so desperately need."

"That barely gives us extra time... which, I reiterate, is hardly sufficient for what you want done. And, I might add, not all my crew will be available to start straight away." She was so young. The observation that she was probably his own age meant nothing. He stared at her hard. "How many projects like this have you done?"

She raised her brow and stared back. "Renovations on this estate house have been progressing systematically. We have had four... five, areas undertaken including the Solarium." There was no way she would confess that her parents organised those. Her idea, her project.

"Fine. Ma'am, I ask that you don't tell me how to do my job."

"If you do your job well, Mr Galloway, there will be no problem. It is my intent that we work together amicably, to ensure everything is completed on time. However, let me assure you, if it isn't, then I have no doubt that my review will mean you will never work in this town again. I don't need to tell you we have many influential contacts. So, let's get along...

26

finish on time, and that way you get your pay and glowing reference. This job will make or break you. I know how important it is to you."

He shook his head, frowned, and put his felt hat on the table. He had been told 'amicable' was something Mrs Bramford could not do. She was certainly living up to her reputation. "Noted, Ma'am."

Joy unrolled the plans. "You have complete access to the work areas. There is no need for your men to be anywhere else in the house at any time. I will ensure these spaces are emptied so you can start immediately." They talked through how they would proceed; where they would store the timbers and the large glass windows that were being delivered. She made it clear that the house and yard must not look like a junk yard, even during construction.

When they had covered everything to her satisfaction, Joy straightened up and extended her arm. Flynn Galloway took her hand. Her handshake was firm. Of course. A woman who would sell herself to a man for a fortune would have to be determined. And when that sale was to a man who was old enough to be her grandfather, he expected she would be resolute and cold.

Joy barely blinked. "I will be available at any time should you have questions Mr Galloway. You may ask Dotty... Mrs Swaine, to come and get me if you need to discuss anything."

"At least if I start straight away, I can get a jump on your timeline. I guarantee you, Mrs Bramford, I will do everything to achieve the timeline we have discussed... amicably." It hardly seemed adequate that he needed to concede this.

Oh. *Mrs* Bramford? Joy swallowed a stammer in her voice as she realised that he addressed her as her mother. "Okay. Good. Well, I will check in every morning routinely." And she abruptly turned on her heel and quickly disappeared inside.

Huh. Flynn ran his hand through his hair as he watched her walk away. He had thought landing this job was his grand break. He could see now why Wilkinson was anxious to pass the job on. He had gone out of his way to give Harold Lincoln a glowing reference on his behalf. Flynn shook his head and doubted the urgency of Wilkinson's family crisis. Now he would have to pull rabbits out of a hat to make sure the work was outstanding, and the timeline was met. At least he had bought himself a little additional margin. Small consolation though.

* * *

5

Joy loved hands on, and she was quite sincere about wanting to work agreeably with the subcontractor. As they went over the plans, she had held her own, and yet, she could still feel his undisguised distain as he turned and looked her up and down. Well. He might be an arrogant, brutish, ignorant and opinionated male, but she would prove to him, that she was not all ditsy feathers, beads, fashionable heels, and Charleston dance-steps. Although she did dance a good Charleston, she noted with a smile. Why she considered it was important to prove any of this to Mr Galloway, she didn't pause to consider.

Joy heard the contractor's truck arrive, and by the time she finished her morning cup of tea, they had already moved in, removed the French doors opening onto the verandah and were pulling off timbers from the outside of the house. The room was to be extended out to where the current verandah railing stood, with a wide bay-window taking full advantage of the views over the garden.

Mr Galloway had a couple of workmen with him, all in worn work overalls. She stood watching as they levered up floorboards on the verandah with a steel bar. The verandah rail disappeared, and they quickly stripped the floor back to the skeletal frame of the supporting bearers.

"You are making short work of this Mr Galloway," she said when he stood up to survey their progress and pulled out a canvas water bag to have a drink.

He stood, balancing on the beams, like a cat on a fence. He tilted slightly when he saw her watching him, but he quickly regained his balance. "The demolition part is quite satisfying. Stripping it back... finding out what we are working with. Your house has strong bones Mrs Bramford. However, be aware that the building stage might seem slow in comparison. So, I encourage you not to become impatient." He still needed her to know that time was not a commodity he could just order from a supplier.

She tilted her head slightly. "Well, Mr Galloway I will not become impatient because I am confident, there will be no need. We cannot afford *slow*."

"So, you keep reminding me," he muttered in irritation. When he turned back to her, Joy had already left. She had other things on her mind.

* * *

6

Joy was satisfied that Mr Galloway, in his man-overalls and heavy boots, would manage the demolition without her constant supervision. She was determined to start painting her canvas. This time, everything about the project was different to what she had done for a long time. The subject was not modern; its style was not trendy. Her intention was not to donate the canvas to charity, or gift it to someone to store in the dusty corners of some attic or even sell it for profit. This mythical commission was just for herself, to hang in her private room. Classic and demure. Personal.

Painting used to be so effortless for her, and she was determined to try and recapture some of that creative flow. She set up her easel and chair in a shady spot in the garden. She arranged a shawl, scrunched in layers, draped over the wrought iron garden table. She adjusted and rearranged the drape again... just so. It took a while for her to be satisfied. Carefully, she positioned a large, green, ceramic bowl filled with the serrated dark foliage of chrysanthemums.

Her father began an annual tradition of picking a bunch of the first blooms to fill her little arms as a child. Chrysanthemums became "Joy's flowers", as if by some divine pronouncement they had been created solely for her pleasure. Her father told her most seriously that 'chrysanthemum' was the proper name for joy... and when all the other flowers gave up flowering, these late-summer and autumn flowers would be there to keep giving the garden happiness. For a little while, a five-year-old, toothless, lisping Joy had insisted that everyone call her "Crissie-thum" because Joy was a name that was too short and too plain. Bennet was mandated to ensure their gardener always had a number of wide beds of these colourful perennials on the sunny side of the garden, that would keep flowering year after year. But for all of their cacophony of colour, Joy's favourite was white. Society gossip said the white *chrysanthemum'* was to be designated as the symbol flower of a newly appointed Mother's Day that the Powers-that-be were planning to include on the calendar next year. Joy did not feel intruded on because it felt fitting. She held this private, quiet ambition that she would enjoy motherhood as much as her dad delighted in fatherhood.

Joy carefully rearranged the foliage in the bowl and adjusted the shawl one more time. This subject was so deeply embedded in her soul, that, regardless of whether it was too early for chrysanthemum blooms or not, she was painting the composition now. She focused on the play of light on the folds of the arranged drape; the iron lacework patterns on the furniture; the shine of the glazed bowl, its colour complimenting the leaves; the shadows around the fringes of the composition. Adding in the flowers would be the very last part of the piece. With her palette in hand, she began to lay down colour, and form, and the fall of dappled light. She knew she could never recreate this particular configuration of the shawl again, so capturing this became the urgent focus of her work for this morning. She was intently absorbed in replicating the shape and shadow on her canvas, and the morning slipped by. Dotty came with a jug of water and placed it on a side table while she kept painting, barely stopping to drink. The shadows of the trees moved with the late morning. When she eventually looked up her father was standing there... with a basket in hand, ready for lunch.

Joy laughed and shook her head. "Are you so convinced that I neglect myself, that you need to bring me a basket lunch like a schoolgirl?"

"Never would I censure you for being a student. My Joy, you know I admire study too highly. A doting father can surely enjoy a picnic with his daughter, however grown-up she has become... and however sick he might be."

She laughed. "You are really milking this story, aren't you? It suits me to allow you to be right. I need to stretch anyway." She stepped back and rolled her shoulders and reached for the sky.

"Will you let me see this urgent prestigious commission you are working on?"

She smiled and shook her head. "I've imagined hanging this picture over the mantlepiece in my bedroom for so long, it is time to get it onto a canvas. When it is finished, the bowl will be full of white chrysanthemums of course."

Her father considered the arrangement on the table with affection. "Ahh, your chrysanthemum bowl. A bowl full of joy. Oh yes. Satisfying subject. Pleasing placement. Agreeable arrangement. Nice."

"Poetic. I'm glad you appreciate my efforts." Joy stretched her arms high again, and then pulled the chairs over to the side table so her father could sit.

* * *

For days, Flynn Galloway sat eating lunch in the shade of the deconstructed verandah, obscured by the piles of timbers, watching them relish this routine of sharing lunch together in the garden over a painting easel. He frowned at the gentle affection he witnessed between the couple on the lawn. This was not at all what he expected. From what he had heard, he considered cold tolerance would likely be the tone of their relationship. He even assumed bold power-plays. But this was not what he was seeing. True, they didn't look like lovers, and Mr Bramford's manner could only be described as paternal, but given his age, that was to be expected. What was unexpected was the laughter. There was fondness. There was comfortable presence. He checked the assumptions he had made and rebuked his bias. Why couldn't this unusual couple have a satisfying relationship as well as any other? Contrary to the gossip-fuelled research he had casually made, it appeared that their relationship was not just a mercenary arrangement after-all. They held real affection for each other. The cold, calculating, clipped Mrs Bramford, who met him on the verandah, was not the same woman on the lawn with her painting easel, sitting having a picnic lunch beside her husband, relaxed and laughing.

He even noticed a twinge of jealousy in his chest. How could their arrangement be so gratifying when his own girlfriend was insatiably unsatisfied? Nothing was ever good enough for Mae. His work, his tie, his hat, his horse, his trade truck, his boots, his contacts and his contracts, were all mediocre in her book. In fact, it seemed that the more he tried, the less he measured up. He found her ingratitude even more bizarre since Mae was a working girl herself. As he watched the two in the garden eating ordinary sandwiches and drinking unpretentious lemonade, he wondered whether Mae had fixated on Flynn as her ticket to a better layer of society and lifestyle. Mae had pushed him to take this job from Wilkinson when he disclosed a moment of self-doubt. A job at the Bramford estate was a high-ticket contract. And in a flash, Flynn realised that he had branded Mrs Bramford with mercenary motivation because he had listened to gossip. All of those stories had seemed reasonable given his experience with Mae.

Oh boy. That was a revelation. Another revelation was the realisation that he didn't want a girlfriend whose whole ambition was to gain an easy pass to society and influence. Mae was young and pushy. He had also met old men, aggressively ruthless in that same quest for more. What he wanted was to be with someone who would sit comfortably in the shadows with him... content. Just as these two were sitting in the shady garden. On the surface they were incompatible, yet reality offered something different. He wanted a life companion beside him, away from the spotlight, just getting on with life and work together. That was the picture he was looking for. Not someone circulating through a crowded room, justifying her flirting to make a better contact, or to secure a better opportunity... to avoid work.

He glanced across at his offsider, Jim, who was quietly sitting in the corners of the worksite, eating lunch. His rough sliced of home baked bread were soggy from juicy slices of homegrown tomatoes. Yet he ate those sandwiches as if his wife had packed a banquet fit for the king and was presiding right there beside him. There was something endearing about Jim's loyalty to her. Mae would never consider packing a lunch, much less sit on the sidelines to eat it with him.

* * *

"Sorry to interrupt Sir... Ma'am," said Flynn, as he strolled over to where the Bramfords were packing up their picnic.

Joy looked at him curiously. She was almost amused that he would take the liberty to interrupt their conversation.

"You said you were available if I had any questions. I was wondering if you had a moment to confirm the plasterboard cornices and features. The order has been delivered, but I am pretty sure this was not what you had in mind. It is different to what was down on the paperwork."

Mr Bramford coughed and stood to his feet. "Well, I am tired, so I am going to retire," he said with a wheeze. "I will leave you two to talk business." He collected the basket and walked back to the house.

"Oh. Okay." Flynn suddenly felt awkward. "I, umm..."

Joy had picked up her paint brush but then paused and put it back down again. Her painting was obviously done for today. She could work on it later in her studio after she sorted this issue out. Now that she had started painting, she was keen to keep the momentum going. Still, she had accomplished most of what she had hoped for this morning anyway. "Of course. I will come and sort it out. I will just pack this away and meet you inside."

"I could carry your easel..."

"Well, if you like." She saw him pause and look at her painting. He thoughtfully considered the arrangement on the table, but he said nothing. "What is it? Don't you like the composition? Does it lack balance?" she asked anxiously.

"No, no... I like it. I do. It just surprises me."

"What surprises you?"

He said nothing.

Joy urged him. "You can be frank. I appreciate an honest critique."

He measured his tone. "I never expected a Bramford, who is set on installing the latest fixtures and stylish décor to host a fashionable Race Week party, would take the time to paint a bowl of leaves."

Joy stared at him in shock, and then suddenly burst out laughing. "It is my great pleasure to shock others with the unexpected. You have given me a wonderful moment Mr Galloway. A bowl of leaves!"

Flynn shook his head as if his ears were ringing. He was not a man given to jealousy, but in that moment, he could deeply understand Mr Bramford's choice in his wife. It hardened a resolve in him that he would not settle for anything less than that picture of sitting together in the shade. He cleared his throat, picked up the easel, carefully holding the canvas so as not to touch the wet paint, and walked back to the house. Joy followed with the bowl, the shawl, and her paint box.

He placed the easel where she directed him and looked around her studio. It was right next to the Solarium. Windows faced out over the back part of the garden "You are very talented Mrs Bramford," he murmured quietly. There were different styles, and a variety of projects. Many of the pieces were poster ready, modern simplistic depictions of graceful figures, looking like theatre-stars, draped in fabric and flowers. That was the consistent theme. She loved flowers. Strange that this new composition was only of leaves.

* * *

7

Inside, Flynn had a trestle table set up with examples of the plaster mouldings and pressed metal features for the ceilings. He cleared his throat and pointed to the array of samples. "The pressed metal features are fine, but I understood the cornice-work and architraves were supposed to be like the European style that is becoming something of a trend. As you can see, what has been delivered is more... basic. Actually, it is exactly the same as what is already in the rest of the house."

Joy stared at them, her mind racing. She saw nothing wrong with these simpler lines herself, but her mother had been raving about the new bold, "jazzier" French style. And she was here, solely to represent her mother's wishes. Just like her father said, *"This is entirely your mother's project."* She took a breath and stepped back into her emissary role. "Can we send them back and meet the deadline?"

"No." He looked away. "I have checked the requisition, and this is what was ordered." He handed her the form where he had circled the discrepancy. "What is stipulated on the plan should have been placed as a special order. The lead-time needed to have that order filled now is well past your deadline." Oh, how he felt vindicated in this moment. Then he braced himself for the tirade to come. Mrs Bramford surely would vent her frustration that this situation had been allowed to happen. It would not matter that the mess up was not his fault.

Joy massaged her forehead and restrained every muscle in her body from running for the hills. "Okay. Okay. This will not do." She took a deep shuddering breath. But as she stood staring at this dreadful deviation from her mother's plan, it was too much, and she fled outside to the garden.

Flynn frowned and watched her pace backwards and forwards under the trees, unconsciously wringing her hands in distress. Something didn't add up, but he didn't understand what that was. Where was the cold and calculating Bramford he met on the verandah? Where was the harsh reputation of a woman that wouldn't hesitate to berate or attack or blame? Why didn't she just try to throw money at the problem to make it go away?

Finally, he could stand it no longer and followed her to the trees. "Mrs Bramford?"

Joy turned and acknowledged him with a nod. She noticed his collar, how it moved with his breath, and as she noticed, the spinning anxiety slowed.

"I'm sure there is something that can be done," he offered soothingly. We can still meet your deadline. I am sure of it."

"But how? There is absolutely no point, replacing cornice work that is exactly the same with what is already there." Breathe. She found herself focusing on the movement of his collar again. "I need it to be perfect."

He adjusted his collar uncomfortably. "It still can be... we will just have to find a different type of perfect that's all. Unfortunately, the original plan of relying on the cornice mouldings and architrave to achieve the styling you wanted will not be possible, given the timeframe."

She paused and realised her anxiety was dissipating. Actually, she had found the smile. She raised her eyes from his collar to his eyes. "You really want to say, *"I told you so"* right now, don't you?"

He grinned. "You have no idea. But I do concede that indulging this satisfaction may not be terribly helpful just now. I appreciate, however, that you are willing to focus on solutions so we can come up with a suitable alternative. Much more constructive than blame."

"Blame? But I do blame! I blame me. I should have had all the orders properly checked. I thought this was sorted, ready to go." The spinning started again, twirling away like a child's toy.

"Well, even though you signed off on everything, I guess some things can slip through the cracks. It happens."

"Mr Galloway, you do not understand. This is not a crack! This is a chasm that will swallow up the entire project!"

"Isn't that a tad dramatic? I'm sure we can sort out something so your end-of-season function will still go ahead as planned."

Joy shook her head, trying to slow the spinning. She took a deep breath again. And her focus dropped from his collar to his chest. Breathe. "You are right. We need to give our attention to solutions. Do you think there is any way this situation can possibly be retrieved?"

"Well... let's go back to your plan. You wanted the new European styling that has strong lines; bold focal features." Yes, Mrs Bramford's plans were boldly contemporary; visually daring; modern. He didn't have any experience with projects like this to draw on. That was one of the challenges that appealed to him about the job. He knew some were saying that he was biting off more than he could chew... presuming to work on a Bramford renovation. When Wilkinson came canvasing, he threw his hat in the ring right away. It was not just the Bramford name that would look good in his portfolio, but the style of this project would showcase the diversity of his capabilities.

"That is exactly what the decorative plasterboard was to accomplish," said Joy with the edge of impatience. "But we do not have those features now."

"You are right. This means we cannot rely on the mouldings to deliver those bold contours."

Joy sighed. How was rehashing the obvious going to help? "Could we use anything else? Mothe... I wanted to move right away from the old-fashioned timber trims that are in the original part of the house."

"What some people call old-fashioned others call classic."

"Not the point."

"Hmm. What we *do* have is simple... plain..." He turned and realised he was standing in the exact spot where Mrs Bramford's easel had been sitting for days. "Plain," he said again, "Blank... like a canvas. You know, I have an idea, but it is a little different to what you had in mind..."

"Please Mr Galloway. If you have *any* ideas, then offer them up for consideration."

"If we don't have to redo the plaster work of the existing room, that gives us margin. So... we can continue the same lines though the room. What if we change the colour of the room to neutral? Like linen... and that becomes the blank canvas for the application of bold colour and the stylized shapes and lines. You would have the same confident features, but they would be painted on. This way you can add anything you want. There could be boarders for some of your own canvases, like the ones stacked in your studio, or painted frieze work. Your function room maintains that feel of consistency with the rest of the house and introduces the modern style you are after. Then... down the track, if you want to change it, your next update will be just a matter of paint and decor, rather than over-hauling the whole shebang."

"Painted features..." She turned the idea around in her mind, rotating the visual like she was circling a sculpture on a stand. Yes, perhaps she could adequately sell this to her mother. "Gold trim looks good with white. And green... like the dark leaves of chrysanthemums. Modern... with a stylish, even classic flare."

Chrysanthemum leaves? There was that unexpected thing again. "Well, it avoids the risk of being old-fashioned. I will engage a designer, so they can run some mock-ups for your approval. A sign-writer can focus on these features. The time saved will absorb the extra work, so I assure you, your timeline can still be met."

Joy closed her eyes thoughtfully and covered her mouth with her fingers pressed together to hide the flicker of amusement on her lips. She kept forgetting that this man had no idea she was just a delegate of her mother with the terrifying reputation.

"You know Mr Galloway, I am going to undertake these designs myself – in the interests of getting the concept started straight away. More margin, and I will enjoy the distraction. So, you can go ahead and confirm your sign-writers."

"You want to do that?" Again... surprising.

"Sure. I will work the mock-ups myself, so we are all on the same page. It will be quicker than trying to describe to someone what I want. And I will paint with the signwriting team. Many hands make light work."

"I mean... do you really want to work on this yourself?"

"This is a Bramford project. Why would it seem so strange that a Bramford would want to contribute? You have already observed that I am a painter of leaves. I wonder that the idea didn't cross my mind earlier."

"You continue to be full of surprises, Mrs Bramford."

Joy let that go through to the keeper... again. She could clarify the title of 'Mrs' later. Yes, she would, of course... but only after most of the work was done. It was convenient that he continued to offer her the diffidence and respect of being the Lady of the House.

* * *

8

Joy worked in her studio for the rest of the day, trowelling through her mother's French magazines, finding the right lines, and the exact shapes, running the stylised theme from the main entry, down the hall and throughout lounge, tying the whole project together.

She showed her ideas to Mr Galloway before he left in the evening.

"Oh. Wow," he said as he paused and raised his brow in appreciation turning the pages in her sketch pad. "Mrs Bramford, this type of design comes naturally to you. You hold a tasteful balance between elegance and stylised decorative features. I admit I was wondering how this approach would work, but you have done it without leaving that feeling of being overly busy. Sometimes I think there is such desperation to be modern that it just ends up looking cluttered, like some crazy second-hand street-stall."

Joy was familiar with praise. People told her what they thought she wanted to hear all the time, but she wasn't after applause. She wanted honest collaboration. Needed it. She had seen a flicker of uncertainty run across his brow when she showed him her ideas. That is what she needed to know about. "I'd appreciate your candour Mr Galloway. But you don't have to moddy-coddle my pride. You looked doubtful when you first looked at the concepts. What was that?"

"I am being quite sincere Mrs Bramford. I wouldn't say I thought it was balanced if I thought it was not. If I have any hesitation... it is the light. You haven't included that specifically. If we feature new light-fittings here and here, it will draw the reflective light up into the room, so that it throws

44

light off these walls. Of course, your chandelier will enhance the high ceilings and drop light from above."

Joy turned away. Of course he was right. She actually thought her mother's choice of a featured chandelier was a monstrosity. It was bold and angular and had none of the delicate features of a classic piece with crystal teardrops. "Is it normal for a builder to be a student of light?"

"The artist in you, surely appreciates that any study – whether oil on canvas or the construction of a building... requires an understanding of light and shadow... especially pertinent in the rooms where we live."

Joy strengthened the dimension of light in her drawings and inserted the light fittings. When she was finally satisfied, she gathered up her concept sketches, and made up a tea tray to take to her father in the solarium. He was sitting in the dark, looking at the stars through a telescope pointing through an open window in the wall of glass.

"The stars are bright tonight My Joy. What a privilege it is to immerse oneself in beauty as old as time. It was Virgil who said... 'The dewy night unrolls a heaven ...'"

"...thickly jewelled with sparkling stars," Joy joined in, finishing the quote with him.

She stared at the sky through the glass panels. Her father was also a student of light. He sighed contentedly and moved his chair around and looked at her puckered forehead in the dim shadows. "How about you tell me what is rolling around in your mind that clouds your face so?"

"Not sparkling jewels of light, that is for sure." Joy launched into her account of the afternoon when Galloway had punched a crater in her mother's plans. She went over to the table and lit the lamp there, smoothing out her bundle of mock-up sketches.

She glanced at his face as he studied her drawings. "Daddy, what should I do? This adjusted concept is our only recourse, given the project has no margins built into the narrow timeline." She paused and shook her head. She sounded like Mr Galloway. "Have I done the right thing? Should I tell Mother about the changes, or make it a grand surprise?"

"Hmm. Retrieving plans that are already crashing, and creating a surprise, are two different things. Don't confuse the two." Mr Bramford sat back down on his day bed, the tea-tray beside him. He poured himself a cup. "I think you have attended to this problem with a great deal of creative work. Are you absolutely satisfied that this offers a suitable solution?"

"It addresses all the design points Mother wanted. Mr Galloway suggested this, and I can picture it in my mind. I think it will be stunning."

"You think... or are confident?"

She tilted her head and shrugged. "Confident? Sure."

"You have to own it. Believe it. Joan of Arc made the forces of France believe her vision because she confidently spoke it out. No apologies are needed for offering a way to avert disaster."

"Okay. Yes, I know this will work. It uses light beautifully and the overall effect will be stunning," she said boldly. "Well, it does now... since Mr Galloway gave his feedback."

"And you believe you can confidently sell this impressive re-modelling of her original concept to your mother?"

"Rationally yes... but she has her heart set on the other. I'm not sure about that..."

"Hmm." He took a sip of tea. "You know... you are bringing this project back from the brink of disaster... one that was not of your making."

"Not sure that Mother will see it that way... even though she signed the requisitions for those plain cornices."

"Ahh. There you have it. The inadvertent mistake. Go and visit the Lincolns. This is a conversation you need to have over a private afternoon tea with your mother."

"Alone? Aren't you coming?"

He shrugged carelessly. "I am in isolation. Consistency is key. Take a copy of the requisitions; don't flaunt them, but the offending documents will be there for her to notice in amongst the others. Choose from these mock-ups, a couple of examples – perhaps this one and this... and make them as detailed as you can, to showcase how this approach will bring that elusive modern European décor to the room. You are Joan of Arc, a humble peasant girl who has crossed gender roles to save France from disaster, leading their army to victory."

"Fantastic," said Joy with a sigh. "Joan was martyred for her boldness in case you had forgotten. I am not inclined to be burned at the stake. Heroism is not my style Daddy."

"Dramatic comparison is used for effect only, not literally. You are startlingly gifted; a modern young woman making a great sacrifice to save this project from destruction. It rests now on how you communicate this dilemma. Diplomacy is an ancient art My Girl... one that paints the problem blackest without blame and then overlays the glittering solutions like *thickly jewelled sparkling stars*. One of the brightest stars in this solution is that we can showcase home-grown Bramford art on our own wildly illustrious canvas."

"Daddy, I think you missed one of the main points when I said this was not my idea. Mr Galloway offered these solutions in a very professional manner."

"Collaboration is a wonderful thing. And if your mother sees Mr Galloway as the glittering star of professional adaptability she will be reassured."

Joy smiled. "I think he will appreciate the elevation to his reputation that this job will bring him. He had mentioned the associated reviews."

"Hold your ideas loosely. They may well be adapted more when your mother looks at them. But to give it the best chance of approval, she needs to see what you can see. You know, it really would be helpful if they came up with a name that adequately describes this decorative style universally. It would be so much simpler." He handed back Joy's sketches.

"A few are starting to dub it 'Art Deco'. Just now I'm interested in showing mother how this will translate into our lounge room."

"Confidence is what is needed. Work on that."

"Thank you, Daddy. You're the best."

He nodded and picked up the volume on French history he was reading. "Oh... and tell Bennet he can retire for tonight. I will stay here for a while yet. This is shaping up the be the most interesting Race Week ever."

* * *

9

Joy walked around the Lincoln Estate gardens with her friend Louisa. "Joy, when I heard you were coming to visit, I was hoping you were finally going to wear those outfits we bought. It would be so nice to enjoy Race Week like old times."

"Old times?" Joy shook her head. "That sounds like I have gone completely AWOL."

"That's not too far from the truth."

"This is the first year I have missed since grade-school... well, war-years aside." She had a roll of drawings tucked under her arm. "Come Louisa, we are best of friends... since pinafores, and pigtails. All I ask is a considered opinion on my drawings."

Her friend sighed. She found Joy's persistent seriousness tedious. Her preferred strategy was to butter her mother up with flattery. Much more efficient. But Joy had lost her inclination for small talk. She didn't talk about boys, or dances, and she avoided all the upcoming Race events with the agility of a circus acrobat. Louisa stopped and sighed. She sat on a bench, while Joy unrolled one of her concept drawings and handed it to her. She explained a few of the key points.

Louisa raised her arched brow and tilted her long neck. "Oh. This is actually really good. The whole room looks like an art-piece without feeling cold, like a drafty old gallery. Pretty clever."

"Thank you. You sound surprised."

"Oh well, you know me... unless there is a man involved, I don't find it all that interesting."

"Funny you should say that. There is a man..."

Louisa's eyes lit up and handed back the drawing with a flourish.

Joy paused, shook her head and retracted. "Yes, and that man is my father. He is there, overseeing my involvement... even when he is unwell. I am chaperoned one hundred percent of the time."

"Oh grief. Your father is so old... old-fashioned."

Joy smiled and quietly murmured to herself. "Classic..."

Louisa rolled her eyes. "Isn't there at least some handsome engineer or something?"

"No engineer. No architect. No baker who delivers our bread."

"Greif. Our mothers have been plotting our escape from singleness since we were babies. Since the war interfered with their plans, I fear that they have truly given up." Her mother's tardiness in sorting suitable suitors, even if a global conflict was the reason, was a great failure in Louise's eyes. It necessitated her taking matters into her own hands. "I have gone out with Freddie Rilston a few times. He has a new motorised car and such a popular way at the clubs. Mother likes him, but Daddy thinks he is too reckless. He says it is a miracle Freddie came back from the war at all. All the other girls are falling over themselves to be noticed by him. Daddy says he hasn't enough business sense, but that is not even true either. He has a great portfolio on the Stock Market. If Freddie doesn't get over the line, I am pretty sure no one ever will."

"Do you love him?"

"Love? Freddie? Hmm, maybe. He is handsome and a great dancer. He has a brand-new car. Perhaps that is enough for me."

"Why let poor business sense, ruin a perfectly handsome face and a sure foot in two-toned shoes?"

"Business is not everything. Life has to be a bit of fun as well. The whole world is still shuddering from the war... and then the flu epidemic. I'm sick of everything being horrible all the time. Why can't we just let our hair down a bit?"

"You don't have to convince me. You know the War broke my world apart." Her heart.

"Oh Joy, I'm sorry. I didn't mean..."

"No, I get it. It is not your fault Joseph never came home. I can still hardly say his name even though he sacrificed everything. I hope the world never sees something that horrific ever again. Father wasn't deployed overseas, but it was such a relief to have him home again. I could not have lost them both."

They sat in silence for a while. Louisa looked at her friend. "Joy, why can't you be more like your mother? It would be good for you to just relax a bit. She has been an absolute hoot while she's been visiting. I sometimes wonder if you were born in the wrong bodies. You should be the party person, and a mother should be all serious and sober."

"None of which sounds at all flattering for my mother."

"You know what I mean... why don't *you* don't have fun?"

"I haven't wanted to for such a long time, but now I have plenty to do. Our definitions of fun differ, that's all."

* * *

"My nerves are positively jumping. What sort of terrible thing has happened Joy dear?" Mrs Bramford puckered her brow and closed the door. She sat down, folding her hands in her lap, facing her daughter.

"Mother, this is something that I fear you will find quite distressing..."

"Oh, my goodness! Your Father's sickness is incurable! Why wouldn't Bertrand come and tell me this in person? That is what this is, isn't it? He is tired all the time, and his complexion is going so pasty. Your Father has sent you here to gently break the news." Mrs Bramford's voice became quite shrill.

Joy considered her mother's fluttering eyelashes. Actually, this was not a bad idea. A terminal illness could make the plastering order seem quite inconsequential. She shook her head, and redirected her mother's thoughts, calmly reassuring her. "No. Of course not. Doctor Bertrand is happy with Father's convalescence. That is nonsense."

"Oh, that is such a relief." Florence looked across her teacup at her daughter. "So, if it is not that, what is it?"

Joy swallowed. "There has been a problem with the supplies for the renovation. Some of the materials which have been delivered, are so far from the original plans, it is a joke."

"We don't have to pay for incompetency or inadequate work. Simply sack Wilkinson and get another contractor."

"At this stage we are already on a new contractor, and since it concerns the plaster moulding, they take time to reorder. We simply can't risk this when Race Week is looming, so we need to use what has been delivered. The positive thing is that they do match the style of the rest of the house."

"Don't let them push you around Joy dear. That is rule number one. Throw some money at the problem, and it will go away. It is very basic business." Florence picked up the folder with the requisitions and flicked through them. Joy watched her closely and noticed she barely paused over the page with the problem order circled.

Her Mother put down the folder and frowned. "So, all that new beautiful cornice work is not available?" Joy confirmed it with a sobering nod. "Huh. That's disappointing. It will mean we will have to cover the plainness with other decorations. That sort of theming is going to take so much longer to set up. Days. We will have to bring the finish date forward significantly."

"Mother, I think I have another solution, which may be more effective than moving our timeline. The fact remains that although we cannot get the original supplies for love or money, the structural work is on track. I think we can do this revised plan without spending extra money because of the savings made on the plaster finishes. Have a look at these concept drawings and see what you think. I believe the end result will be unique and stylish."

"Hmm," she said noncommittally as she picked up the sketches and scanned them. "Did you discuss this with your father?"

Joy nodded. "Yes, he wanted to know what you thought."

"Well, it seems like you have worked this idea thoroughly. Hmm. I think I like this much better actually. The style is still bold and invigorating. I love the colours... and the way it ties into the rest of the house. If we go this way, we won't need any extra staging at all. If you can get the tradesmen to pull this off, you will be the star of Race Week, without setting foot on a racecourse."

Joy sat back and took a slow breath. She couldn't believe the sense of relief that she felt.

* * *

After dinner that evening, with crystal clinking, wine flowing, feather boas waving, music from the gramophone blaring, Joy sat in the Lincoln's sitting room and watched the gathering, detached from the conversation and banter. She reminded herself that these excursions into her mother's world, were the price she was required to pay if she was to step outside it at other times.

Louisa sat beside Freddie Rilston, frowning impatiently as her father bemoaned yet again, his inability to source reliable timber supplies. Harold Lincoln's one reoccurring headache was this problem of inconsistent deliveries. This issue was limiting his ability to take full advantage of the post-war building boom. Freddie looked restlessly around the room, supressing another yawn as he reassured Mr Lincoln of his sympathy to his plight. Joy felt she could finally excuse herself when everyone started reviewing the horse line-up for Race Week, projecting the rise of a true champion. It was a relief to say her goodbyes. As she opened the door to her automobile, a voice behind her came running to her side. "Joy, wait..."

"Oh. Freddie..."

He brushed his hair out of his eyes that were a little glassy from too many wines. "That was as boring as shovelling stables. Just putting in my dues. Hey... since you are Louisa's friend... I wanted to ask... could you put in a good word with her parents? Mr Lincoln is determined to blacklist me, and I know they respect your family immensely."

"Freddie, I think you overestimate my influence."

"Sure... but you know how he goes on and on about the building supplies... It gave me an idea... you know, since you are renovating your place... if you knew of... Mr Lincoln must see that I have..." He faltered, losing his train of thought.

"What? What do you have Freddie?"

"Aww, I don't know... some sort of solution."

"Do you have a solution?"

"Well, no. But that doesn't matter. I just need to look like I have one. Would your father know someone who could come up with something? It would make such a difference to Mr Lincoln's opinion of me."

Joy paused by the open car door and noticed disappointment stir in the pit of her stomach. Freddie had no interest in a real solution but wanted the kudos of one. Evidently Mr Lincoln also saw that as well. "I could keep my ear to the ground in the chance that something comes up. I'm pretty busy at the moment, so I am not sure I can help."

"Well, thanks. I am grateful anyway. Louisa's right, you're the best," he crooned, his charming manner smoothing over the roughness of his request. Since Louisa liked polish and veneer, Joy could see how her enthusiasm for Freddie was like a kettle on the boil that was about bubble over.

Joy got in her Austin-7 and drove off. This car had been a birthday present. Deluxe. British. It was important to her mother that Joy own an automobile – it showed spunk and prestige, especially as a woman. It was important to her father it wasn't an American car, and they held loyally to their British heritage. Mrs Bramford love affair with cars now meant that any eligible young man, should at least, be able to match her interest in cars. One enthusiastic buck went so far as to buy his own motorised vehicle, even though he refused to learn how to drive it.

When Joy drove through the gate at home, Galloway's truck was in the driveway. "What is he doing here?" Joy murmured as she watched him pulling out timber beams from the back of the tray.

Joy sought out her father and reported back about the interview. She kept it brief, sat back and shook her head. "Galloway is out in the driveway unloading timber. It is Saturday night. It's late. He should be at home... with his family."

"Seems he has chosen to be here instead. Why don't you ask him in for a night cap?" her father suggested with an air of indifference.

"Huh. Good idea." She went out to the truck where Flynn was still dealing with his load.

He jolted when he saw her. "Oh, Mrs Bramford I thought you were... You look... umm... like... you have been to a party." Stunning.

"Hmm. I have. But I am home now. Fa... Mr Bramford was wondering, since we were going to have a light supper... if you would like to join us?"

"Oh... well, I guess." Anything to distract him from the afternoon he had. He had finally spoken with Mae. She had been angry. Very angry. But the only detail he could recall from the conversation was his overwhelming sense of relief. Actually, now that he thought about it, he hadn't eaten all day. "Supper sounds nice; I forgot to have dinner. And lunch. I'm just about finished unloading. Will be in shortly."

"Forgot?"

"Yes, well... I have this very important contract that consumes all of my attention." That was only partly true. Mae had burnt up his energy like a firestorm. He felt beat. But the way she flew at him in a temper, only cemented his determination to follow through. To do something as routine and mundane as unloading timber created some space in his head. Planks didn't yell back.

"So, Mr Galloway, it seems that you have all the timber you need," said Joy as she passed him a tray of savoury finger-sandwiches, muffins, meatballs and slices of quiche. "Have you had any delays in getting your orders filled?"

"None. At least not for a while. It used to be a bit of a problem." He took some of the meatballs and put them on his plate beside his sandwiches. He considered his coffee and added some sugar.

Mr Bramford thoughtfully sipped his drink. He noticed with amusement that when he suggested a simple nightcap, his daughter went to all the effort to pull together a supper in league of a Race Week smorgasbord. "How's that?" he said. "Lincoln is constantly saying Wilkinson has terrible trouble with supplies since the building boom has taken off."

"Simple enough. I've hired my own lumber crew. I've got contacts with property owners who need clearing. My crew fell the timber and local sawmills run it up. When I don't have to deal with third parties, I reduce the likelihood of delays."

Joy swallowed. That was some pretty serious work-around. Did she really want to advocate for Freddie just now? "Freddie Rilston said Lincoln would appreciate a reliable timber source. I wonder why he hasn't approached you about it?" she asked with a raised brow.

"Probably for the simple reason that I don't advertise. This is my solution for the same problem I had with supply delays. This is at least one variable that I can control. I am a builder first; the timber-getting is only a sideline to support that." He said it blandly, but he glanced at Joy, and he could tell she got his point. He quite capably anticipated problems and proactively put solutions in place.

"Mr Lincoln would take as much timber as you can mill. Have you thought about expanding that side of your business?" said Mr Bramford.

"No. Like I said – a sideline."

"Well, perhaps you should." Mr Bramford drained his glass and stood up. "I'm off to bed. I've had an exhausting day. Joy will update you regarding the new plans."

Flynn watched him leave with a furrowed brow. It was like the man was giving him every opportunity to flirt with his wife. "Joy?"

"Yes: my name. Means happiness."

He cleared his throat. Well, that was patronising. "So, is there is an update? You know that every change is going to impact our timeline. What exactly have you changed this time?"

"Nothing really. Only that what we talked about regarding the cornice work has been given the stamp of approval. Ahh... what I mean is... I am comfortable to proceed now."

"Oh. Good to know. I thought it was already sorted."

"Well. I just wanted to think about it some more."

He noticed her awkwardness, cleared his throat, and dove into logistics. "Okay. Well, I have spoken to the signwriters in town. They have a crew available, so I have booked them. We need them working on this virtually at the same time as the painters finish the walls."

"I've already told you that I want to work on the features myself."

"I know. And I thought about that. Given the short timeline, and the detail we require, the crew will do all the pinstriping and frieze boarders around the cornices. That way it leaves you to focus on the artistic features. That stylised flower shape you have running through the whole theme is so unique, I would hardly trust anyone else to do it. And I had another idea..."

"Like what?"

"Well, the wall beside the stairway... is so... well..." he shrugged.

"You can say it."

"It is the only space that has no real 'oomph' to it. And I wondered what you thought about..."

And by the time he had finished talking, Joy had already grabbed her pad and reconfigured her ideas. It was late when he said goodbye, and Joy went into the studio for a little while longer to capture her inspiration on her pad.

* * *

10

Joy went for her morning walk around the grounds picking some spring flowers. What Flynn had identified as dead space beside the stairwell, had now become the feature wall. The flowers in her arms were to help her add in some detail. As she walked the loop back to the house, she passed Flynn's truck parked in the driveway. The dew over the hood and windscreen, indicated the vehicle had been parked there all night. She tapped on the cab door window.

He jolted upright and sheepishly slid down the glass, staring stupidly at her. Her arms were full of dew-drenched flowers, looking like some mythical woodnymph in the morning light.

"You stayed out here all night," she observed.

He blinked hard and cleared his throat, still rough with sleep. "I ahh... do have a swag. Had it set up on the tray... but I bailed when there was a shower of rain. This was dryad... dryer..." He cleared his throat awkwardly and rubbed the sleep from the corner of his eye. Woodnymphs. Faeries. Dryads. They all fitted.

"Mr Galloway, don't you have a home?"

He looked at her and said nothing.

"Well?" she persisted.

"I am... in between residences at the moment." He shrugged and wondered what she would think if she knew some of his story... the private version, rather than just the contracted construction part. "My girlfriend... ex actually... didn't want me staying there. We parted company yesterday."

"You live with your girlfriend?" she asked in horror.

"Not anymore..." He wondered why he should care if she was scandalised or not. This woman did nothing to hide the fact she had sold herself to an octogenarian for the security of a fortune. "She was just letting me stay there until I found my own place... while I took this job. I'm not from here. I came in on short notice on Wilkinson's recommendation." He shrugged uncomfortably. "It became obvious that the temporary arrangement identified some permanent problems, so I..." He shrugged.

"Greif. You look like death. Come inside before anyone sees you camping on our doorstep like a stray cat. Have a bath and clean up. Why didn't you say anything last night? We have guest rooms."

"You would hire me a room? That would actually solve a lot of problems for me. I could work late and start early. Mrs Bramford, if you are serious... I accept."

Joy cleared her throat and raised her eyebrows. She wasn't actually offering Bed and Breakfast, but... "Oh. Well, if you think this will help the renovations... I will check with Mr Bramford."

"Of course."

* * *

Mr Bramford came to the dining room, in his dressing gown and sat at the table, while Dotty placed his egg and toast down in front of him. She offered another serve to Flynn, plonking the china plate very firmly in front of him. He said nothing and just continued eating. Mr Bramford poured his tea and discretely tried to look indifferent to the sudden appearance of one of the workers at the Bramford breakfast table. After a few mouthfuls, he looked up with a reflective crease on his brow. "You're starting early Mr Galloway."

Joy jumped in. "I have suggested that Mr Galloway rent the guest room. That way he can start work early. It's on the other side of the house, so it should not disturb you."

"I don't feel disturbed... just curious. This is an uncharacteristic approach to managing renovations... having the builders move in."

"Our timeline is uncharacteristically demanding. You were the one who set the timing of the work. I am just operating with what I was given."

Flynn studied his eggs with intensity. She obviously had not checked with her husband, and it was awkward they were talking about him as if he wasn't in the room. More evidence their relationship was more complicated than he was led to believe.

Mr Bramford drank his tea, salted his eggs again and ate slowly. "Once again, My Joy, it seems like you have come up with a considered solution. As long as Mr Galloway here, doesn't mind seeing me before my morning shave, or you with sleep in your eyes." Although he did notice that Joy was dressed immaculately this morning. No slippers, no pins in her hair.

Joy shook her bobbed short hair and flashed her startling green eyes. "I'm pretty sure... that by the time the renovation is completed, Mr Galloway will be familiar with more than just my bleary eyes." Flynn choked on his toast and gulped his coffee. Joy calmly drank from her breakfast teacup, and then paused as she replaced it in the saucer and continued to direct her remarks to her father. "I have decided that I am going to do some of the feature painting on the walls myself. It is like working on a larger canvas. This way I will be sure that the work is done to my satisfaction."

"Your devotion to this project is really quite commendable My Girl," said Mr Bramford without even cracking a smile, and not even Joy detected his amusement over this idea.

* * *

Contrary to Flynn's projection that the structural part of the building would be tediously slow, it was not long before the roof line was adjusted, the wide bay-windows were installed, and the new floorboards were laid. The electrician came, then the plasterer; the window seat was built in; the cushioned seats were delivered by the upholsterer. They stood wrapped and stored in her studio. Soon the painters would start, and then final sprint to the line was polishing the floorboards. It seemed the normal sequencing was compressed, and everything was happening at once.

The signwriting team arrived, with their ladders and paint splattered aprons, clutching their clusters of brushes, and their wooden mahl-sticks with the leather balls on the end. Joy reviewed the layout of the whole decorative plan with them. She had three canvasses hung in the hallway that required ornate boarders to be painted around them. She replaced them with blank canvases before the work began.

The crew were allocated areas and started painting with their brushes, resting their wrists on their mahl-sticks that were positioned against the wall, propped against the front of their aprons or locked under their arm. With extraordinary accuracy, their fine intertwining lines were simultaneously delicate and unyielding, creating ornate borders of leaves along the architraves and cornice work. Joy followed along behind them with her own palette, adding in the stylised blooms to the interweaving stems and leaves. The work streamlined the whole area, adding a burst of colour to the gold and dark green borders.

When it became too crowded among the ladders and the signwriting trestles, Joy escaped to the shadows by the stairway and painted... and painted, absorbed in the process of creating something from nothing. This was the largest canvas she had ever worked. A wall lamp had been installed, casting light down over the wall, transforming this drab, uninteresting, bland space into a feature that was vibrate, colourful, full of energy. Joyful.

In the late afternoon shadows, Flynn adjusted an additional lampstand so that it shone on the wall at just the right angle where she worked. After a while he came back. "Everyone else has gone. Don't you think you should take a break?"

"I am very nearly finished... there is just a little more to do..."

"I know. Please take a break. Perhaps if you took a walk in the garden, it would refresh you some." He reached out and offered her his hand.

She nodded and took his hand without even realising... and as she stood, he held it for a moment too long. Suddenly he pulled away.

Joy took off her apron, walked to the door and turned around. "Why don't you come with me – this was your idea. You could do with a break as well."

They walked in silence for a while. There were so many things he wished he could say. Instead, his voice was stiff and formal. "Your art is remarkable Mrs Bramford. Your hard work is bringing this project out from the shadows making it outstanding. Your Race Party will be something special."

"Oh well. You know what they say: 'A good venue is essential for a good event'." At least that is what her mother would say. "I am just doing my part."

"The polishers are starting on the floorboards tomorrow. We can still do some finishing detail after that, but it needs the full week to cure before we move your furniture back in... which will bring us to Thursday. Congratulations Mrs Bramford. You have successfully met your timeframe..."

She smiled at that. "Down to the wire; we made it." Joy had thought her original idea to paint her canvas in the garden during Race Week had been ambitious. Now she realised she would have been so bored if that had that been the entire scope of the season. Even possible, that in craving distraction, it may have even driven her back to the racing events, as tedious as they are. This had been so much more to her liking. Joy had not thought about races and cocktail parties the entire time she had been working. And she had painted and painted and painted. "Thank you, Mr Galloway. Thank you. This has been the best Race Week ever."

"Oh? I had thought the sacrifice required to miss the festivities was disappointing."

"Oh, not really. I have done Race Week my entire life. This has been a welcome respite."

He frowned and raised his brow at the same time, distorting his expression. "Well, I'm told your reputation as a hostess is famous."

She really didn't think he had any idea about her mother's reputation. After all, he still believed her charade. "Well, you will be able to tell me if it meets your expectations firsthand. Of course you must come."

"Come to your party? Why would I come?"

"Because our guests will want to meet the person who has worked the transformation of our living room."

"Aren't I a little bit contractor, working-class?"

"Mr Galloway. That is harsh. We have worked together since you lifted that very first floorboard. Besides, it is expected you will come if you want your reference."

"Are you holding me to ransom for what was already agreed? You said you would write a reference if you were satisfied. Aren't you satisfied?"

"Of course, but I need you there in case our guests have technical questions regarding the work."

"Humph. Then I guess I will be there... if you say so Mrs Bramford."

Hmm, she needed to address that. Now. "Mr Galloway, I wanted to clarify something. It has been a matter that I have wanted to speak with you from the start, however, it seems that..."

Dotty's voice sharply cut through her speech, calling them in for dinner.

Dotty's unbending disapproval was not easily put aside. "I am pretty sure your Mrs Dotty Swaine does not like me." Protective of her mistress no doubt.

"She's been with the family a long time. I think you handle her well enough."

"I doubt Mrs Swaine is one to be 'handled'. But this is your project, so I focus on what you want done. I think we make a good team."

"I think we do too," said Joy thoughtfully as they turned to go inside.

"What was it that you wanted to clarify?"

She had a whole week. She would do this later when Dotty wasn't breathing down their necks. "Ahh... only that I am going to work late tonight. I don't want to leave all the detail on the wall until after the floors are done. No need for you to stay up just because I am."

"There is always something to do. I'll assemble the chandelier; it needs to be ready for hanging when the floorboards are polished."

＊＊

12

The music from the gramophone played its jazzy tunes. Lights shone on the featured paintings with a soft glow. The chandelier dominated the room with its tiered sparkling geometrical crystal stalactites. Some couples danced, while other guests lounged on the long window seat filled with cushions, and others mingled holding their stemmed martini glassware like trophies. The spacious area was transformed into a dance floor surrounded by a gallery. Featured glass figurines stood in lit recessed alcoves; tall flower arrangements filled in the corners. Groups clustered about admiring the trilogy of hanging frames along the wall, bordered with intricate gilded and green pinstriping that were fine like lace and stiff like wire. Stylised flowers and leaves intertwined the fine lines, like weeds in a mesh fence, so it was difficult to distinguish which were the stems and which were the wire. The wall by the stairs featured the same stylised flowers, which had escaped the stiff wire borders and split over and transformed into a joyous field of realistic wildflowers dancing with butterflies.

Flynn noticed it all with a bemused sort of satisfaction. He stood by the wide French Doors that opened out onto the verandah. He was gazing through the generous windows, overlooking the garden that flickered with light from the border of fire-torches. Groups mingling comfortably around the garden in the warm November weather.

Wilkinson came and stood by him. "Got to give it to you Galloway, this was a pretty bold gamble. A make-it or break-it type of gamble. Makes a flurry on the horses look kind of tame... even for Race Week. Seems like it paid off though. *The* Mrs Bramford is one happy little bunny, bouncing all over the place. That is not an easy thing to achieve. Here's to you, mate," he said as he thumped his shoulder and raised his glass to where Mr Bramford presided over the room, standing in front of the sleek geometric mirror that flanged out behind him like a fan. It gave him the look of a Pharoah presiding over his kingdom.

"Oh, that was not what you..." Flynn glanced across the room and paused. He cringed as he watched a woman come and fawn over him with a familiar air of presumption. "Who is that lady on Bramford's arm?"

Wilkinson frowned. "Who do you mean?"

"There... with..." he paused as Joy appeared. Dressed and sparkling, making her way comfortably through the fashionable crush of people. His forehead puckered in confusion as he watched her greet both Mr Bramford and this other woman with a kiss. Were these people arrogant enough to flaunt an open relationship?

"Her?" Wilkinson nodded. "That little glittering gem is their daughter..."

"Daughter?" Flynn's frown deepened, as every interaction over the past weeks flashed through his mind. *Mrs Bramford* indeed!

"Yes. Her name is Joy, and she is aptly named. Most eligible listing if ever there was one. But you won't get near her. The mother is fanatical about the type who would presume to get an introduction."

Flynn titled his head and said nothing. His mind racing.

Wilkinson thumped him on the shoulder again. "Wouldn't that have been the icing on the cake, if you had bumped into her while you were working here? But not surprising you didn't though, being Race Week and all. Socialites are rarely at home. Well, your luck has run out now. That horse has left the starting gate, and you are just bringing up the rear, covered in dust."

"Hmm." He shrugged carelessly, studying the trio. "I was only introduced to Mrs Bramford."

Wilkinson grinned. "And yet, here you are... still standing. Well, done mate. That is a win, bigger than this week's Cup. I think I can take at least fifty percent credit for this success, since I gave you the opportunity in the first place."

"Sounds to me that you were throwing me to the wolves Wilkinson. Wolf. Mrs Wolf."

Mr Wilkinson's grin broadened and lifted his glass tumbler filled with ice and rum. "Never mind the horses. Here's to you... running with wolves." He took a swig of his drink and left to talk to another mate about the final highlighted race.

Flynn could not take his eyes off Joy. His world was undergoing a seismic shift. Her dress sparkled and her eyes danced. She had a bejewelled little fascinator in her hair, gems and pearls that flashed in the light, softened by feathers. She was the royal princess standing beside the King and Queen... talking graciously with those who hovered to offer homage. He could see the resemblance with her mother. A flatterer might even call them sisters.

Joy caught his eye and tactfully extracted herself from those monopolising her attention. She inconspicuously made her way over to him, smiling through the room, like one of the butterflies flitting around the field of wildflowers she had painted by the stairs. After some time, she landed by his side. He felt the flutter of her presence like a shock wave. "Well Mr Galloway, your ideas are in the spotlight this evening, just as much as my art-pieces hanging on the wall. We will be happy to give you the glowing reference you asked for. Come, I would introduce you to my mother. She is, after all, the one who signs off on your work."

He didn't move. He was trying to balance his rage and his gratitude. He said stiffly. "I think I would like to finally meet *Mrs* Bramford, Ma'am."

"Joy. You can call me Joy. Our official work here is complete."

"*Miss* Bramford will suffice," he said tersely as he offered her his arm and they moved through the crowded room.

"Warning," she whispered with a smile to the people they passed. "My mother can be quite frightening. I know because even though I love her dearly, I have lived with her intimidation my entire life." She guided him towards where her parents were standing.

"Hmm. She is not the only one who can be intimidating... *Miss* Bramford. Perhaps it is a family attribute, like the colour of your hair."

"I do appreciate your discretion, Mr Galloway," she returned formally, looking straight ahead.

"My conduct through this entire project has been completely professional. I don't intend to throw it away now. I need that reference."

"Of course... the reference."

"Succinctly put," he said quietly, with a charming smile, and a voice of ice.

"Mother, I would introduce to you the master builder who worked our renovations. This is Mr Flynn Galloway. My father you know, Mr Galloway."

Mrs Bramford turned towards him, taking in his modest suit, thoughtfully "Oh? I specifically requested that Wilkinson work on our project."

"Wilkinson wasn't available, Mrs Bramford. He had a family crisis at the last-minute," said Galloway as he stuck out his hand.

"You seem too young to be a master builder," she said looking him over. She didn't take his hand.

He put his hand in his pocket. "When I took the job, Mr Bramford was sent all my references."

Mr Bramford nodded calmly and took a couple of glasses from a circulating tray. He handed one to Flynn. "And they were exemplary, I must say. We were fortunate to secure him, My Dear, given the urgency of our time frame."

Joy picked up a toothpick skewered with olives, pickled onions, and cheese. "Exemplary references," she echoed, as she tasted the olive. "It is true."

"There seems to be so much about this job, that I hardly know about," Mrs Bramford said with a frown.

"Mother, I told you about the supply debacle. You said you were satisfied. Fortunately, Mr Galloway kept his head, and we met our timeline."

Mr Bramford nodded sagely. "And that My Dear, is exactly the point. Can you imagine how the stress of all this would have interfered with the management of your Race Week responsibilities? As it is, you come tonight as the glowing hostess of this wonderful party with a relaxed mind, able to enjoy the evening with our friends. That was our gift to you, even if it is not tied with a ribbon."

"But of course, James, of course. How thoughtful you are." And she grazed his cheek with a kiss, and turned towards her other guests, gushing about the highlights of Race Week, and soaking in the compliments of their spacious room that was so improved from last year.

* * *

71

13

Someone changed the disc on the gramophone and a particularly catchy number filled the room with its lively tune. Joy looked around that the couples who were already dancing... toes in, heels out, twisting and shaking in time. "This is my favourite song to dance to," she observed casually. It was a less than subtle opening that any socially awkward dullard could drive a truck through. Mr Galloway had a truck. Joy started tapping her foot.

Flynn stood unmoved and nodded to Mr Bramford. "Excuse me Sir..." he said, and he bowed out. He walked through the open French doors onto the verandah and rested his forearms on the rail, looking out over the garden. Torches were flickering in the shadows, weirdly dancing in time with the music. How many times had he wanted to talk to Joy as *Miss* Bramford, when he was led to believe she was married. Now he was fully aware she was single and eligible, yet she was more unavailable than ever. All those rehearsed internal conversations dissolved in the mild November warmth of the evening. He heard her step behind him, her tread familiar to him now, but he did not turn.

"Everyone is happy with the renovation. Mother is very pleased."

Joy's voice washed over him like the balmy breeze from the garden. Their first meeting flashed through his mind. How harshly he had judged her when he had assumed she was Bramford's bride. A simple explanation would have corrected the misunderstanding, yet right from the beginning she had refused to offer one. He swallowed and spoke out into the breeze. "I am glad that the Bramford family is satisfied." His tone was formal, and he could feel his forearms stiffen.

"Please Mr Galloway... I wish to explain."

He straightened up and pursed his lips as he turned. "Explain what exactly? I think I understand the situation well enough now. What I thought was collaboration was really you adjusting the spotlight." She offered no apology, he noted.

"That is what I need to clarify. If you will not dance, please, come for a walk with me in the garden. There are so many people out and about, we will hardly be noticed. Just another couple going for a stroll. Please... let me say what I need to tell you."

"You are mistress of this house, and it seems that I am still here to do your bidding." He offered her his arm stiffly and tried to seem indifferent about the whole matter at the same time. They walked down the stairs out into the shadows lingering around the fringes of the garden.

"It distresses me that you are so annoyed. You are right to be, I guess..."

"You guess?"

"But we have worked together so amiably, and our collaboration has achieved such remarkable success. Everything you prophesied about the problems associated with our timeline have proved to be correct."

"I hardly think I would call plain common-sense the gift of prophecy."

"The renovation really does take full advantage of the view of our garden. Our guests are no longer condemned to stare at walls, knowing there is a garden just beyond them. See how the two spaces merge so effortlessly. This is thanks to your work. I have told people this."

He shook his head doubtfully. "Your mother had all the plans drawn up."

She insisted. "True. But you get full credit for the creative take on this renovation."

"I don't want 'full credit' – that's the point. This was a collaboration; it was teamwork. It was the *working together* that was so effective. together. You said that yourself. Or so I thought. I didn't even know who you are *Miss* Bramford."

Joy stopped and took a breath. "I didn't actually lie about who I am..."

He raised his brow and again felt his arms flex and go cold. "Really?"

She sighed and continued walking. "I know I allowed the misunderstanding to persist. I even encouraged it. But that is because Mother's reputation helped me have the courage to do this. Initially I thought the project would be a simple distraction, a decoy. Something I could use for the sole purpose of avoiding all the palaver of Race Week. I just wanted to paint! And Father thought the experience of supervising the renovation would provide a valid excuse to allow me to side-step my mother's incessant matchmaking."

"Doesn't alter the fact that you misrepresented yourself to me."

"I know Mr Galloway, but even if this is my first renovation, it is not my first rodeo. Men notoriously dismiss women without giving them credit for sensible thought, nor consider their ideas worthy of common regard. My mother has learnt to overturn those ignorant roadblocks by her severe and intimidating manner. It was easy to ride in the current of her reputation."

He considered her in the flickering shadows of the torch light as they walked, unmoved by her explanation... but unsettled by her voice. How was it that the tone of her voice rattled him?

"The project was supposed to be a clean and uncomplicated way to give me time to paint," she repeated. "But right from the start it was not what I thought. Wilkinson wasn't available. You sub-contracted. The orders were incorrect. Simple things swallowed up our margin of time. Suddenly we were immersed in trying to prevent this whole thing from sinking like the Titanic."

"All of those things were manageable. And we dealt with each challenge as it presented itself. *We* did those things Miss Bramford. *You* and me. Not your mother. I was not the only one who kept their head. You had the presence of mind and courage to make every decision as it was required."

"That is generous of you Mr Galloway. We do work well together."

"And yet... even when I had proved myself not to be one of those brutish types you so fear, you still hid behind your mother's reputation. Did I really come across as so unworthy of your respect?"

Joy stopped and brushed her eyelashes with the back of her gloved hand. It disturbed her that he persisted to accuse her so harshly. Why wouldn't he just smile and dismiss it as a misunderstanding? "Mr Galloway, I am sorry. I do respect your good opinion. Otherwise, why would I go out of my way to seek your forgiveness?"

"Miss Bramford, I don't know how I can wholeheartedly trust your word in any matter again."

"You can! Let me prove it to you!"

"How can I know that what you tell me is real? What other fictional circumstances might you create to baluster your faltering self-confidence in your artistic reputation? Well, this will be very impressive in your portfolio."

"That is unfair. I have said I have given you credit." She shook her head, despairing. "I told you my mother was intimidating Mr Galloway, but

I would have you know, *you* are ten times more severe. For those who know my mother, that is really something!"

"Again... how would I know? I only have an imposter to compare her with."

She gasped in shock and pulled away from his arm, quickly turning back towards the house.

"Miss Bramford, wait..."

Joy paused and blinked her eyes hard before she turned around. "What?" she said sharply.

He came and stood in front of her. "I sincerely agree with one thing that you have said: we work well together. I concur with that wholeheartedly."

"Thank you," she murmured.

"It is expected that your mother's party will generate interest in this style. I anticipate others will want to replicate some of your ideas that are showcased tonight. Miss Bramford, would you be interested in working on another such a project, if it came up? If I had your terms, I could work your consultancy fees into the quotations."

"Does this mean you forgive me Mr Galloway?"

"It means that I am open to creating another opportunity where we can trial working together again. It remains to be seen whether we can work as equals, without your mother's trump-card always sitting in your pocket."

"I never used it!"

He raised his brow sceptically. "Yes Ma'am, if you say so."

"Why would you ask me to consult if your confidence in me is so tidal. Look at what we accomplished together! We did this! Why do you doubt we could replicate such a collaboration?"

"Like I said... it remains to be seen *Miss* Bramford."

She tilted her chin. "Then sign me up Mr Galloway. I will prove that I have every capacity to be part of your team... as me... not my mother."

He reached into his vest pocket and pulled out a card. "Now you have my details, Miss Bramford. I will contact you if another opportunity arises that may be of interest." He bowed stiffly and returned to the house to collect his hat and coat. He called it a night. There were too many people, even outside, and the raving reviews all seemed too numerous and too shallow to be genuine. He wondered if the reference he so jealousy sought would be worth the paper it was written on.

* * *

14

The door opened. "I am here to meet with Miss Bramford," said Flynn standing on the front step, formally, holding his hat.

"Who is it, Dotty?" called a voice from inside.

"Mr Galloway, the master-builder, Mrs Bramford."

"Oh, bring him through. He is here for his reference. I will just have to write it out. Won't take long."

Dotty took his hat and deposited him in the loungeroom with a frown. Flynn blinked and resisted the urge to rub the back of his neck in his nervous state. He cleared his throat as she turned to go. "Mrs Swaine... Dotty... could you tell Miss Bramford that I wish to speak with her please?"

Dotty turned her eye and dropped her chin. "The work you were brought in to complete, is finished."

"Miss Bramford said that if I needed to speak with her, that I could ask you. Her wishes surely still stand. I am here on a business matter. Not personal."

That sounded more reasonable. Dotty pursed her lips, unimpressed. "Very well. Wait on the verandah." Somehow having the tradesman outside made this deviation from the Bramford protocol less provoking. He had no right to sit at the breakfast table to start with.

He complied with a nod and stepped onto the verandah. It suited him to be here. The room, even with its sweeping views, was too busy with all of its decor, and visual movement... even in the morning sunlight. It felt like it was trying too hard. The best part of the whole thing was Joy's paddock of painted wildflowers by the staircase. The new style was too stiff and unnatural for him... even though every critic had affirmed they had captured 'that perfect balance'. No, he preferred plain, simple, calm... even sparse. He felt himself unwind as he looked over the garden. Trees. Grass. Life. He heard her step behind him.

"It seems every time we meet, it is on this verandah, Mr Galloway," Joy said. Her voice unnerved him. It felt like a summer breeze. Like joy.

"Perhaps that is because I prefer the outlook over your garden without the glass. It is the closest thing in the city that reminds me of the bush. It relaxes me." He turned and his eyes connected with hers. "All that it needs... to be perfect, is a cow chewing its cud, a horse with a foal, or perhaps some geese grazing near your pond."

Joy laughed. "I'll see what I can do to accommodate your ease Mr Galloway. I'll even add a pig to wallow in the water fountain. But not geese – their hissing frightens me... perhaps a duck or two. Quacking is friendlier. I like ducks."

He smiled. He had wanted to shock her. All that she did was to run with his idea... and deepen it. He had witnessed that phenomenon when they worked together many times. He said nothing for a while, and then he straightened up and cleared his throat. "I mentioned having you consult on some work with me. I have been offered to quote on a job for the "*Majestic Grand*", the new theatre being built over on Horseshoe Bend."

"That is one of Mr Lincoln's larger projects. Are there problems?"

"Not too many. The construction is on track and just about done, but Lincoln wanted to revamp the interior design after attending your mother's party. He didn't feel that their majestic interior was grand enough."

"Majestic and grand is a lot to live up to."

"They have the premiere of the movie "Sunshine Sally" on the sixteenth of December. If we take the job it needs to be ready for opening night."

"Oh. That soon. That makes Race Week seem like a stroll."

"I'm sure it can be done. But only if you are on board. I do happen to know that tight timelines are your speciality. I wouldn't consider it otherwise."

"You are going to manage the interior design of the entire theatre? That is quite a shift from building an extension for a private residence."

"I can do logistics, but I need your artistic eye. If we can rework their current plans to give it a bit more pizzazz, then the job is ours. Some things we will have to go with... like the seating. And obviously he won't replace the carpet that is already ordered. Just come and have a look before you say no."

Joy looked at him and tilted her head. "You assume I will say no."

"Just come and have a look with me."

"When?"

"Now."

"Right now?"

He grinned. "Absolutely. Right this second."

"Well okay. But only because my curiosity is burning holes in my head." He followed her through the house, and they took their hats from the hallstand by the front door. Dotty appeared like an apparition, tracking their every move.

"Dotty, tell Mother I will be back for lunch. Mr Galloway will collect his letter of recommendation then. We will take my car."

"Mrs Swaine," said Flynn, nodding farewell to Dotty. He stepped outside and stopped mid-step on the wide stairs and turned towards her. "This is *your* car?"

She smiled with a shrug.

"Of course it is. Miss Bramford would own an automobile just to create a reaction. Trust I didn't disappoint."

"No, perfectly adequate. I am driving."

He nodded and grinned. "Of course you are."

They pulled up outside the construction site. Men were scaling scaffolding and painting the wide bricked arches built into the facade over the entry columns leading to the foyer.

Joy stepped out of the automobile and took it all in. She closed her eyes. If this was the opening event of some stage play or concert, what would she expect the interior of a majestic and grand theatre to look like? Patrons would be buzzing with anticipation, tickets in hand, dressed up for the outing. Moving pictures should be allocated that same sense of occasion as live theatre. The equipment required to project the images meant that this type of entertainment could never happen in a living room at home. Going out needed to feel exclusive, opulent, special. She imagined the voluptuous drapes, the stately marble columns framing the stage, muted lights down the side of the hall. Then there was the foyer... pinstriping around where movie posters would hang. It would hold the same sort of line-work they had incorporated into their living room but without the softened floral emblems. No – these swirls needed to be bold, regal, like a royal invitation on linen pressed paper, embellished with the imprint of a wax seal. Majestic and Grand.

Flynn turned and watched her curiously as he stepped up to where she stood. When he started to speak, Joy put up her hand, and he fell silent. Her mind was still scanning. Large hanging classic chandeliers, potted plants and wide armchairs, scattered occasional tables to invite people to cluster for civil tête-à-têtes. Ushers in uniforms: men with bow ties and waistcoats with blinking brass buttons; women with smart heels, wide collars and flattering bows. Colours would be royal blue, regal red, and of course gold. Gold paint, gold trims, gold tassels. Gold. Yes gold. Lots of gold.

She opened her eyes and smiled at the look on his face. "I wanted to get the picture in my head before I am bombarded with wheelbarrows and sawdust."

"Do you need more time?"

"No. I have it now."

"Okay Ma'am. This way please." He offered her his elbow and she took it with a skip. They picked their way around plaster buckets, ladders, frames, and trestles.

"Galloway! You came. So, you are going to take the job."

"Depends, Mr Lincoln."

"Depends on what?"

"On her." He indicated the girl on his arm.

"Who?"

"Sir, I believe you know Miss Bramford."

"Joy! What are you doing here?"

Flynn nodded with a sober air. "Mr Lincoln, you are looking at the creative genius behind the elevated magnificence of the Majestic Grand."

"People told me you did the reno. If she is the 'creative genius', what am I paying you for?"

"We work together. We have the ability to transform this theatre into something that will be monumentally magnificent. A fitting legacy, Mr Lincoln, to bestow on your community for years to come."

Mr Lincoln's frown did not abate. "Oh, I don't know about this. You'd never see a Sheila in a sheering shed or part of a shipman's crew. It's not right to have a woman on a construction site either. It's not done. Does your mother even know you are here Lassie?"

Joy didn't flinch. "Sir, I think a better question is: *Who will give you the best result?* As Mr Galloway has identified, we have the means to deliver what you want: Majestic and Grand."

"No disrespect Joy, but it is going to be a distraction to have you tripping around, flashing your heels, dresses, feathers and beads!"

"Then Sir, I will simply come to site in overalls."

"That's ridiculous. What lady would do that? This is a far cry from the hats of Race Week. My Louisa wouldn't be seen dead in trousers."

"Respectfully Sir, my work is the only issue being assessed here, not my friendship with Louisa, nor my attire."

Flynn cleared his throat and pointed to the very plain stage area, still under construction. "Miss Bramford, would you like to explain to Mr Lincoln, how you envision this part of the theatre? What will it be like if we are given this opportunity?"

"Absolutely..." and she started to describe the sense of occasion, the experience that would immerse each patron. She spoke of the grand aspect of the stage... framed with sweeping deep red, gold trimmed drapes... drawing every eye towards the magic of the silver screen. The plain supports that were lying in front of the stage would be transformed into imposing stately marble columns, created by the illusion of paint work. The cornices would encompass dimensional plaster work features, added to create visual interest and depth to the goldwork. "When people go out to a theatre, they are looking for an experience that allows them to escape into the mysterious world of extravagance. It becomes a portal to another world. That is the experience of theatre... we capture that and embellish it. Every patron's line of sight will always be invited to look up and forward. Every line, every stroke of colour is about drawing their vision upwards. It is same in the foyer. Chandeliers that sparkle and sprinkle light everywhere. Pressed ceiling features detailed in gold. Long drapes falling from the ceiling to the floor in that same rich red. Each contour draws us up into the cathedral ceilings, leaving us immersed in grand and majestic."

Mr Lincoln blinked. "Pardon the French Miss, but I can't afford that."

Flynn smiled confidently. "But Sir, I think you will be surprised how this extravagance will not be expensive. You've already allocated money for our services. It will take some budgetary adjustments, but it will not be outside a reasonable investment. Let me draw up the costings. You will not be disappointed."

"Well, okay then. You make that happen... and I won't mention her dresses," he said as he put his hand on Galloway's shoulder and ushered him into a side office.

* * *

15

"Oi! You, there! You can't stand around having smoko all day. If you can't do your work... you can always find another arrangement."

One surly character spat on the ground. "You're right about that! I can always find another job." He threw his cigarette to the ground with some verbal emphasis and ground it with his heel. "You think you are somethin' strutting around with your swanky big-fella threads. I don't have to put up with this!"

Flynn watched him leave with a couple of mates. The other men shuffled uncertainly but stayed. A couple of them stubbed out their smokes.

"Anyone else?"

No one shifted. "Then back to work."

No one moved.

"What's going on?"

One worker tentatively cleared his throat. "Mr Galloway, Sir, the bolts for the seating. They didn't send enough."

"That's it? You are standing around because you don't have bolts?"

A few nodded. "Come on guys. I can't read minds! What have you done to fix this?" Flynn zoomed in on the young man who spoke. "What's your name son?"

"Simon James, Sir."

"Come with me James. Since you spoke up, you seem like you have the where-with-all to help solve this." He had been on the lookout for a someone with foreman potential. Simon seemed like a likely candidate.

It was the end of the day. Joy had a smear of gold on her cheek, and her overalls were splattered with paint. She was packing up her paints and set them aside to roll up her drop-sheet. The shadows in the theatre were growing dim. Flynn flicked on the floor lights, and their soft glow filtered across the carpet. "So, tell me Miss Bramford, are you confident we are on-track for opening night?"

"You have told me many times that logistics are your forte. You know if we are on target to meet the deadline or not."

"Ahh, but my question was whether you actually believe we will make it. The drapes are being delivered tomorrow. That has been the major hold up. Your doubt has been ongoing. Surely you have some confidence now."

This had been more stressful than any home renovation. "If I have seemed anxious, it is because there is a lot more at stake here than a social gathering in our living room. You confidently say it can be done... but I am aware that any number of things could still go awry. You barely averted a full mutiny from within the crew."

"We are better off without them. In a very short time, Simon is proving himself a loyal team-player. He is keen to improve himself. I think he will go far."

Joy was amazed how Flynn always managed to find the up, the positive, the optimistic side of a situation. She pointed to a gramophone sitting on a box. "Why would you allow Simon to have music playing while the crew is working? Wilkinson would never allow it on his worksites because it is distracting. I wonder if he has a point."

"There are a couple of things that went into that concession. Simon now has more credit with the crew. It shows them that he has initiative and will speak up to improve things. Did you notice that the seating was installed in a day when they have been messing around with that job all week. Besides, music may seem like a distraction, but it fills in the gaps and reduces the swearing and bickering. On the most part, it has created a more amiable environment. A very adequate workaround I would say." He paused as he considered something. Eventually he tilted his head. "Miss Bramford... do you know why I didn't dance with you at your Mother's Race Week party?"

"Because you were mad with me. The cold-shoulder was your way of exacting revenge." Not swooning for the privilege of a dance with the hostess's daughter got her attention at least.

"Perhaps I wanted it to seem like that, but actually there was another matter that was standing in my way... and I haven't figured out a work-a-round for that particular problem yet."

"Oh? That is quite a confession for the person who has a solution for just about anything."

He nodded and shrugged and took a risk to bare his soul. "Fact is, I do not dance. Cannot. Never learnt. I didn't want you to know that in front of everybody."

She stared at him and then burst out laughing. "Oh my! The agony you put me through! You are the only man I have ever met who was not falling over himself to be my dance partner. Here I was thinking that you were furious with me."

"Oh, I was mad, make no mistake. But the dancing was a convenience. Perhaps I have not been straight forward with you either. Now however, now... oh how I wish I could dance with you now."

"Really? Are you asking to dance with me Mr Galloway?" He was forgiven. That was certain.

"I would if I could. I really would."

"Well, you ask... and we will dance."

"But..."

"I will teach you."

He paused and swallowed. "Okay... Miss Bramford, will you do me the honour of this dance?"

"It would be my pleasure..." She went over the gramophone sitting on the box, and chose some music from the box beside it, and then she stepped up to his outstretched hand. He followed her quiet instructions, stepping around the stage. There were a few awkward moves, and some gentle laughs as she continued to guide him through the steps. "I think you are a natural dancer Mr Galloway. If we continue to practice, you will be a very confident partner in a very short time."

He looked down at her in his arms and grinned. "I disagree. I don't feel confident at all. I am going to need lots and lots of practice."

* * *

Flynn sat on the edge of the stage and looked over his crew who were gathered lounging in the seats still shrouded in their dust covers. "I want to thank each one of you for the work you have done. The time we had to pull this job off has meant long hours, but we have managed it. I have organised a special thank you for your effort." He paused for effect. "We have an exclusive pre-release matinée screening of *Sunshine Sally* on Thursday, at 2pm. As you know, the movie premieres on Saturday, so only your immediate family can attend with you. And I need signed confidentiality forms from everyone to confirm absolute assurances that there will be no talking about the movie until after opening night. If I have your word on those matters, we can go ahead."

There was a general murmur of shock and smiles. New theatre, new moving picture, new everything... and it was a work crew... *their* work crew, along with some of the ushers and staff, who would experience it first.

* * *

16

Flynn walked with Joy, past the arches and the columns, down the wide stairs out into the sunlight on the street. They blinked to allow their eyes to adjust to the bright light after the dimmed theatre. "So, what did you think?"

"People are saying that the theatre is indeed Majestic and Grand. I think we have met the brief." Admiration lit her eyes. "I still can't believe you organised an exclusive matinée just for our crew."

"Well, it will get around that we had the private showing. The mystery of the movie is still intact, and our crew will be more loyal and work harder... and it cost me barely anything. That sort of good-will is priceless."

Joy smiled at the excitement of the workers as they emerged with their families. "Mr Galloway, this was an outstanding gesture."

"Seems you caught me out. Perhaps you concede I am not ignorant and brutish after all.

"Oh please! Will you ever get past that?"

"Well, I am considering it," he said with a relaxed grin. "This actually had a dual purpose. It was also a way I could take you to the movies... without all the palaver of Opening Night. You told me that you don't particularly enjoy that type of thing. It would be Race Week all over again."

She glanced at him and could feel a flush run up her cheeks. "So, this was a date?"

"How could it be a date? I haven't spoken to your father yet."

"Yet?"

"If I were to ask you on a date, it would be appropriate that I speak with your father first."

"Oh." Her heart sank. Flynn Galloway would never get past her mother's eligibility-screening. He was a blue-collar worker just starting out. In that moment Joy realised that she really wanted him to pass the Bramford pre-date selection rituals.

"Miss Bramford, would you join me for a celebratory stroll. Just a quiet way to mark our magnificent success. I might even include ice-cream," he said with a grin.

"Well, Mr Galloway... you are full of surprises. Sure... if you are offering ice-cream." He directed her towards the parklands overlooking the bay. They stopped at an ice-cream stand, and he bought them each a cone.

Flynn caught the drips of ice-cream that trickled down his fingers in the summer warmth of December. "We could talk about the movie if it is just between us. Do you dare tell me what you thought about it? To be honest, I'm still not terribly comfortable with the idea of moving pictures telling a story. I think I prefer a book so I can turn the pages at my own pace."

"Well... it was very strange having our city up on a screen. Unnatural almost. I think it would be easier if the story had been set in some fantastic imaginary place like what Jack found when he climbed the Beanstalk. And they used words like "*Cobber*" and "*Bonza*" and "*Blimey*" ... and getting married was '*getting hitched in a double harness*'. Who even talks like that?"

"Just about everyone I know..."

"Humph! It wasn't realistic."

"And his proposal! '*I jes bin thinkin'... two kin live as cheap as one...*' That was a very crass way to propose, if I have ever heard one."

"I think that's the point. I thought it was funny... as did everyone else... in case you didn't notice."

"And I think there was something quite discordant about a story set in the poor streets of Woolloomooloo, being screened in a theatre that we worked so very hard to represent the 'majestic and grand' side of Sydney." The ice-cream was gone, and Joy fanned her face in the heat.

"You don't seem to remember that you are from Potts Point yourself. You don't get nicer than that around here. At least in the end, the characters were rescued from the common streets of Woolloomooloo, and they all lived reformed lives."

"Really Flynn? That's your idea of a happy ending? That Sally marries her wealthy, handsome lifeguard and escapes mediocrity by getting a better address?"

"I think self-improvement is admirable," he said.

Joy shook her head. "I am all for improvement, but when those lovable reprobates, Spud and Skinny, finally reformed... it didn't feel sincere."

"That's true. When Spud gives up the drink, his temperance was reluctant, and it had nothing to do with God. He just wanted to live out his days with his pretty Salvation Army lass. The story seemed weak at that point."

"Mr Galloway, if you were given the artistic license to change the story, how would you write differently?"

"I would write it back to front. Instead of the well-to-do hero rescuing Sally from the surf at Coogee Beach... and then rescues her again by teaching her the etiquette needed to fit into the flash part of town, in my version, the rich guy would be rescued by his working-class lady. Perhaps he would go to live in Woolloomooloo... and live a simpler, less pretentious lifestyle. He could join Skinny in hawking rabbits from his horse and cart; they'd make a thriving business partnership – Skinny's charm and his business sense. The girls have already lost their laundry jobs so they would open a thriving millinery shop, making rabbit-felt hats. Their happy ending would be independence. A working partnership, flourishing on hard work and initiative."

"You surprise me Mr Galloway with your thinking. I pegged you for being more traditional. However, your version still needs a rescue. It's just that your liberator is a woman, even if she is from the ordinary streets. Why should we be rescued by another anyway? Why can't we make our own choices about what we do?"

"I think we all want a story with a rescue and a happy ending because it rings true of our own story. We can't escape it."

"My father has told me my entire life that clear thinking, ingenuity, and grit is what changes our circumstances, not a rescue. He often reminds me I don't need a knight in shining armour to fight my battles. He has always encouraged me to stand by myself."

Flynn grinned. "But what if we do need rescuing. It may not be from squalor of the unsociable suburbs, or the evils of booze like Spud in the movie."

"What are you getting at Mr Galloway?"

He took a breath. "I'm thinking about what I read this morning about the blind man wanting to see. Everyone has a level of blindness. No one is exempt."

Joy frowned. "Mr Galloway, are you quoting the Bible to me? Are you are going to start preaching on an upturned soapbox? I didn't see that coming."

He paused in the pace of his step. "So, if I introduce an idea from the oldest, most reliable moral source in history, it becomes street-preaching? I actually think it is a valid reference point."

Suddenly their walk and their talk had become uncomfortable... and she didn't really know why. Perhaps she just didn't want to talk candidly about something so serious. At least, not with a man who worked in overalls, and sat beside her at the movies. That was too strange. She pursed her lips and said nothing. They walked for a while in silence, along the path through the shaded parkland.

"Flynn... I need to tell you something."

He noticed the sober shine to her green eyes. "Sure. Did you want to sit?" When she nodded, he guided her off the path and they sat under the shade of a tree. What other secret had she been keeping close?

"Um.... I... I used to be engaged. His name was Joseph. We were friends all through school. He was the perfect boyfriend for someone from Pott's Point. He was the love of my life."

"What happened?"

"He was deployed to Egypt and didn't come home. It wasn't even enemy fire. He got some middle eastern fever."

"I'm sorry... that is hard."

"I don't usually talk about this. So, you see, when I say... no rescuer... I guess that comes from my experience. Nothing and no one is a sure thing."

Flynn shrugged. "True... but that is a desolate reason to stay away from others. Perhaps it is not about one person rescuing the other, but more like a dance... learning to step in time, and to keep rhythm to music of life. Talking like this feels like that sort of dance practice to me. I could not discuss anything personal like this with Mae."

"Mae?"

"My ex. She really wanted to be from Potts Point and she thought I would take her there. It was exhausting trying to meet her expectations."

"I am not used to talking so openly about things that are usually private. You are the only person I have really allowed to get close since then."

Flynn shrugged. "Ahh. See. It takes practice. Your frankness is a very endearing quality, Miss Joy Bramford. Brave even."

Joy flinched. He had not used her first name before. The sound of it on his lips was... beautiful. For the first time, she didn't feel that her name was too short or too plain. Her heart swelled, quite unexplainably. And what she noticed was the absence of fear.

"So, Joy, back to the movie... do you think, that 'Sunshine Sally', is the Aussie response to the American movie 'Pollyanna', like some have been saying?"

She appreciated that he wasn't going to interrogate her on Joseph. "Well, I guess. They both are about someone who, in spite of hardship, finds the silver-lining. Which version do you prefer?"

He grinned. "I think that you are trying to tear at my loyalties. If I had to choose between Yankee or Aussie culture, I would obviously cheer on our own. It is like asking someone to wear different footie colours. You just don't go against the code."

"But consider the content of the art... which do you think has more to say?"

"I've seen the Pollyanna moving picture as well, but I prefer the book. If I could say it without demeaning our own, I think Pollyanna's Glad-Game is quite remarkable. She changed lives where she lived, with gratitude. Not sure our Sunshine Sally had the same impact. It was just about her own escape from mediocrity, and she didn't really contribute much to that in the end anyway."

"But it is insulting to be called 'a Pollyanna'!"

"Of course... and people prefer bread-and-butter pudding to plain bread and butter. But I happen to like the taste of pudding. Pollyanna had real challenges to confront. Her habit of gratitude made the difficult sweeter."

Joy laughed. "You are going to break out in song and start singing '*Count your Blessings*' now, aren't you?"

Flynn grinned, "Always appropriate to follow a good sermon with an uplifting hymn."

Joy shook her head. "You are full of surprises, Mr Flynn Galloway. So full of surprises."

"You didn't expect that I would read children's books? Or go to the theatre? Or sing in church?"

"Not really. No." She laughed. "No... not any of those. Not from a chippie from Woolloomooloo."

"Well, I had help with the books. My cousin is a bookworm. And she talks to me incessantly about what she gets her students to read. She demands that I read some of those books, to get my take on them. I would not have been able to have this conversation without her coaching."

"I think I would like to meet her. She sounds like a good influence on you."

He grinned again, stood up and offered his hand to help her stand. "She is. Yes."

* * *

17

Bennet ushered Flynn into the solarium and left him there. He turned around, scanning the corners of the lush foliage. He tentatively started to look through the hothouse, and it took him a while to locate Joy's father in the back corner.

"Mr Bramford?"

He was potting some orchids on a table, that was partitioned off from the main walkways by a large classic oak bookcase, that was stocked with all sorts of tools and potting supplies. Mr Bramford glanced up. "Oh. I have a visitor. Or is this business? We are not ready to start further renovations, if you are intent on drumming up another job Mr Galloway."

"No... I... I wanted to talk to you about a personal matter."

"Oh? So, visiting. Visitors usually come to attend my wife. Or my daughter. I rarely rate a mention. Mostly that suits me."

Flynn stood awkwardly watching him work, but he didn't move.

"Hmm. Give me a moment then. I'm nearly done. Here – hold this pot while I transfer this. I like the texture of dirt. Feels... grounded. I like to think that my attempts at propagation are promoting life and growth. Perhaps I could have been a farmer in another life. Still, it would never do to just grow a potato. No... far too ordinary, even though I admit I am the first one to feel neglected if I don't have a potato on my plate every night. Orchids, however, are different. Orchids are too glorious to be common. This pastime allows me to dabble in cultivation without the humiliation of ordinariness. So, I stick with orchids. I agree with Ralph Waldo Emerson who says that *'Flowers are a proud assertion that a ray of beauty out-values all the utilities in the world.'* I guess utilities would include potatoes. What utilities do you want to discuss this afternoon Mr Galloway?"

"Actually, it was more about the *'ray of beauty'.*"

Mr Bramford looked up again and studied his face but gave no hint that he had any idea of his meaning. "Are you looking to go into orchids?"

"Maybe. I pretty much would turn my hand to anything at this moment, to secure some favour in your eyes."

"Oh, don't be so easy," he scoffed. "My daughter deserves someone who will stand on his own worth. You don't have to cultivate orchids to do that."

"Oh. Has she spoken with you about us?"

"Not at all. I have been given no indication that there was even an *'us'.*"

"Oh. Of course not, Sir. I assured Joy that I would speak with you, before asking her out. As would be proper."

"If proper is important then perhaps you have gone about this all back to front. You refuse to dance with her at her mother's Race Week party. You come to do our renovation but end up enlisting her to do a lot of your work. You conscript her onto your blue-collar payroll. You think nothing of placing a lady of social standing into a common work crew. You would even include her in a charitable screening of a moving picture with all sorts of labourers, so that Joy told her mother she had no inclination to attend the premiere to see it again. None of these things are the usual approach to courting my daughter, nor anyone else of her social calibre."

Flynn frowned. Everything the man said was true. Hope faded about ever dating his daughter. He stood there holding the pot.

Mr Bramford started on his next orchid. He said nothing for a long time, focused intently on the root-ball in his hand. "I notice all of these things, including one other matter of particular significance."

More hope drained from Flynn's face, leaving his colour quite pallid.

"So, no curiosity? At all? Don't you want to know what that is?"

He put down the pot where Mr Bramford indicated with a sweep of his trowel. "Yes Sir. It may help me understand the situation better."

"Well, I would say – don't change a thing. I have never seen my daughter happier. Joy is suddenly bursting with a creative fire, which has been forced for quite some time. There is a lightness about her just now. If you are contributing to this monumental shift in my daughter's demeanour, then you are my friend Mr Galloway."

"Sir, does this mean you would consent to me dating your daughter?"

"Perhaps I would. But that does not mean that you will be able to do this just yet. You see, I may consider these observations in the light of some virtue, but I seriously doubt that Joy's mother would. So, unless you can convince her mother, you may very well never have the opportunity to take Joy out on a real date. Ever."

Flynn's heart sank even further. "How would I even know where to start in navigating such an obstacle?"

"I suspect you wouldn't have a clue. But fortunately for you, both Joy and I are practiced at enlisting support from her mother."

Flynn didn't know what to make of that, and he reached for his hat that was sitting on a ledge.

"Wait here. Joy usually makes an appearance around four-thirty. We can discuss it with her then. You can help me here until then." He handed him another pot. "Waiting shouldn't be too hard since my daughter is one of my favourite topics. Tell me... why are you so convinced that you would like to date my daughter?"

"Well Sir, she is the most stunning combination of talent, kindness and intelligence I have ever seen. She is independent and speaks her mind. When I am with her, I am compelled to be the better man. To be honest, I find some of her ways frustrating, but I am driven to work it out, as it is impossible for me to walk away. I think these things are the 'ray of beauty' I find in her... like your orchids. Perhaps those exquisite blooms are more like her, than the common chrysanthemum that she tells me is her favourite flower."

Mr Bramford studied the root ball in his hand. "You have made my daughter your study. That was very well rehearsed."

"Rehearsed? Oh no Sir. I'm sorry if it sounded forced – that was quite off the cuff. My rehearsed speech was very different."

"Well, you could not have answered in a better way. Since you put so much thought into it, did you want to give your rehearsed version now?"

"Well, it was more about how I might be a suitable person to take her out. I have every means of supporting her."

"Supporting her? How much effort does it take to support one date?"

"Sir, you must know... I am seriously considering taking this further."

"Hmm. You are pretty bold for a chippy." Mr Bramford was amused, and his eyes shone behind his rimmed glasses. "Tell me about your meeting with Mr Lincoln..."

Joy did arrive at four-thirty. She bounded into the Solarium. "Daddy?" she called out, "I really need to talk to you about something important. I think that Flynn Galloway... Oh." She stopped as she rushed around the corner to the potting table and blushed brightly.

Mr Bramford had lined up his orchids along the table. "We are found. I think Mr Galloway has beaten you over the line. He has been quite forthcoming. But before we start on what he has been saying, I need to ask: do you have any reservations about his overtures?"

"What do you mean?"

"Are you willing to date him?"

She gasped and stuttered for a time. That was direct. "I... of course. But why all the..." she stopped, not able to put her finger on the right word.

"Well, you and I both know this will be a manoeuvre more intricate than Race Week. I am not going to all that bother if you are not really interested." He studied her face and then shrugged. "Okay. Well then. Let's not delay, otherwise Mr Galloway here, will be greying around his temples before you both ever go on a date."

"Daddy, you would help us?"

"No. Help would reek of manipulation and interference. I am simply supervising my daughter's interests as a concerned and cautious father. And I can see that you are interested in Mr Galloway here. Very much."

* * *

18

Mrs Lincoln smiled and graciously extended her gloved hand. "Merry Christmas Mr Galloway. Flynn... may I call you Flynn? I am so glad you were able to come. My Harold told me you were coming."

"I'm glad to be here Mrs Lincoln. I appreciate the invitation. Very festive."

"Well, it does come around so quickly. The sooner we get in the festive mood, the better. My Harold has been singing your praises like a choirboy. I'm considering revamping our dining room."

"I'm honoured to be considered for your renovations. We should talk further sometime."

"I agree, let's not get immersed in work tonight. Allow me to introduce to you Louisa's friend, Freddie Wilston. He...". She never finished the introduction as the cook appeared, flustered, and vying for her attention over a crisis with the menu, so she rushed off to attend to the calamity.

"Freddie." Flynn extended his hand. Freddie was dressed to impress, and his flashy get-up matched his flashy smile. This is what he was competing with. He felt himself cringe, and he did not feel at all up for the task. They were ushered into the living room where drinks and appetizers were circulating. "I understood the Bramfords were coming tonight," Flynn commented casually as he watched the stream of guests coming in the door.

"Oh, they had trouble with Joy's car. It hasn't been the most reliable thing." That explanation came from Louisa who hovered around Freddie like a honeybee. That felt back to front to Flynn. Wasn't the lady the beautiful flower in any courtship?

"Well," said Flynn with a smile, "perhaps they should have kept their horse and buggy. Reliable at least."

"Greif man, these motorised cars are taking over the world. I have an Auto. No one who is anyone keeps a horse now-a-days."

"I'm all for advancement. As long as it gets you to dinner on time."

"And don't forget that a shiny new machine does make a good impression. We can't deny that now, can we?" He flashed his eyes at Louisa, who giggled her approval. "It is only right to be able to appeal to the ladies." He grinned at Louisa again, who smiled coyly in return.

"Reliable is enough for me. Especially when there is no..."

"You know... the stock market is the way forward, my man. If you did that you could afford to buy your own car, just like me." And he proceeded to sprout his wisdom on this all-consuming passion of his, with a fair smattering of condescension. "Stocks are the currency of the future, my man."

Flynn nodded and phased out. He wondered how a comment about a reliable horse and buggy became the natural segway into a stock market analysis. As he watched Freddie talk about his portfolio, reliable was not the feel he was getting from his whitened smile and his two-tones shoes. He'd rather work the old-fashioned way. His timber crew had Clydesdales, heavy draft-horses needed to negotiate forestry terrain and the distances. He sold his horse, a beautiful animal with sort after bloodlines, trained for both the saddle and harness, to buy his truck, but he had every intention of owning a horse again, when he could. On the most part Flynn was a practical man. But even if it was not very practical, his love of animals was one of those indulgences he would allow himself. Not to impress anyone. Just for him.

His truck was a practical acquisition. It was well used. It was reliable... on the most part. But you still had to feed it, and shoe it, and groom it, although those routines looked different on a machine.

There was a flurry at the door as Mr and Mrs Bramford arrived. Joy followed them inside. There was a great deal of gushing and hellos and apologies, and the music went up a notch as couples began to dance. Flynn felt his heart leap, and he turned away so he didn't disclose himself. They had contrived a plan for Flynn to demonstrate his capacity to engage in this world. He was to have at least a couple of dances with Louisa. But Freddie had quickly acquired Louisa's hand, and it didn't seem like Flynn would get the chance to dance with her after all.

He was relieved when Joy finished her greetings and retreated to the shadows on the fringe of the room. Flynn picked up a drink and handed it to her. "You don't seem to be too interested in all of this merry-making, even when dancing was part of our strategy for this evening. Are you bored with the festivities already?"

Joy sighed. Just because her name was Joy, it seemed to create this expectation that she would be into every sort of frivolous celebration. "It is a little too much, I think. Just an extension of Race Week. I feel that my time would be better spent at home painting, regardless of the reassurances that Father felt this evening would serve our cause."

"I was told this occasion would be a quiet, private affair."

Joy smiled. "This is what *private* looks like in the world of Harold and Eliza Lincoln."

"Ahh. The spirit of Christmas.'

"Still, it does not feel like this is the most appropriate way to celebrate an event that started in a rustic shed with a baby and a few sheep-farmers visiting."

He looked at her eyes and grinned. "I have to say that on that point, I couldn't agree with you more, Miss Bradford. Christmas is a reverent occasion; more than what this is being offered here."

Smiled and sipped her drink as she scanned the room over the rim of her champaign glass.

"I have a question for you Miss Bradford."

She continued to scan the room. "I'm listening..."

"I was wondering if you feel that the dance lessons you have given me would be sufficient for the teacher to put the student through his paces."

She grinned into the crowd. "Are you asking me to dance Mr Galloway?"

"Yes, I am. But only if it doesn't clash too severely with your moral loathing of the occasion."

"Well, I accept. It may actually serve to buffer my misgivings and help me engage... goodwill and all that." The music quietened to a gentle waltz.

"Let's do it then, since I *was* encouraged not to avoid the dance floor. Plenty of time to dance with Louisa later." Flynn extended his hand, and they walked towards the middle of the room. As he placed his hand on her waist, the music screeched to a holt. Freddie raised his glass and tinkled it boldly with his twizzle-stick.

"It seems our dance will have to wait," Flynn sighed regretfully as Joy stepped back and a glass was pressed into her hand.

"Ladies and gentlemen, may I have your attention," said Freddie with his confident smile. "While I have the lovely Miss Louisa here with me, please join me in raising your glasses to Mr and Mrs Lincoln in appreciation for their hospitality tonight. Merry Christmas everyone!" Louisa blushed, smiling gloriously over the room, as she raised the glass that miraculously appeared in her hand. Gathered guests scrambled to take a glass from the circulating trays and raised it in a toast. Many *'Merry Christmases'* echoed around the room, with the clinking and chinking of glassware. When Louisa turned back, she gasped. Freddie was on one knee beside her. "Miss Louisa Lincoln, would you do me the honour of becoming my bride? Will you marry me?" he asked breathlessly.

Every eye was on them. Men frowned. Ladies raised their brows in shock. Flynn glanced over at Mr and Mrs Lincoln. Louisa's mother was beaming, and Mr Lincoln stood beside her frozen with a forced smile. Mr and Mrs Bramford stood unmoved. Joy blinked. If it wasn't for Freddie's flashing grin, she thought he could have been negotiating stock bonds and calculating dividends. But then, perhaps he was. Freddie was one who was willing to take a risk and expect the stock exchange would clearly show the payoff at the close of business each day.

Louisa's dramatic pause had everyone holding their breath. "Yes! Oh yes! Of course, yes!" Louisa finally gushed with a flutter. There was a collective sigh. Someone raised their glass higher in congratulation: "To Louisa and Freddie!" The champaign flowed again. Lace handkerchiefs were produced from purses to start dabbing the makeup around the ladies' eyes. Christmas was off the table, and in a moment the evening transformed into an engagement party.

The music resumed, and Flynn took hold of Joy's hand. "I think I need that dance now. Pretty sure I will not get any time with Louisa tonight."

* * *

The guests were gradually leaving. Freddie was outside, lingering in the warm December evening, drinking in the glorious success of his surprise. Joy came and gave Louisa a hug. "Congratulations my friend. And you were worried about Freddie not getting over the Lincoln line."

"Oh, Mother was never the concern. It was Father. We planned the whole thing. We figured that if we sprung it in a public place, he wouldn't have to endure speeches about working your way up. It was just perfect. Aren't I just the accomplished actress? No one had the slightest idea I wasn't surprised. I was just swept off my feet in a starry-eyed moment. I could go into acting on the silver screen. In fact, I might."

Joy forced a smile. "I am happy for you Louisa." Her friend's 'perfect' arrangement had effectively put a spanner in her own romantic schemes. Any opportunity for Mr Bramford to highlight Flynn's virtues, subtle enough for his wife to overhear, was swept away with the spotlight on the surprise announcement. Freddie got a full proposal, and Flynn was as marooned as ever on the wrong side of the Bramford suitor's island.

* * *

19

"Galloway. Glad you could come. I have something I need to discuss. Sit down."

"Yes, Mr Lincoln."

"First, I must express my disappointment."

Flynn scanned the theatre job in his mind, beginning to end. He was here to collect his final payment. "Sir, you received gushing reviews on the Majestic and Grand in the newspapers. We met your deadline. What are you disappointed about?"

"You. I expected more from you. I expected loyalty!"

"What on earth are you talking about? When has my loyalty ever been questioned?" Had the defectors from his crew spitefully planned a counterattack?

"Every day it seems. You know Wilkinson has had trouble sourcing reliable timber, and it has come to my attention that you have your own lumber crew."

"Oh. The lumber."

"Yes. And it was Freddie who told me about this. It amazes me that you wouldn't volunteer this information, or that you would not offer to contract for my jobs."

"It is only a small crew, and I am loath to be another source of frustration for you Mr Lincoln. I am not in a position to consistently provide the amounts of timber that you require."

"Rubbish! I know you would meet each delivery in full and on time. You have that way about you. You met the Theatre deadline without a hitch."

Flynn raised his brow at that. There had been plenty of hitches.

Lincoln pulled out a contract and pushed it over to him. "I am offering more than I give my other suppliers. This will solve a lot of problems for me. Why don't you come to dinner with us for New Year's Eve – you know, a bit like the Christmas do. This is not the official work one. Just a private, quiet evening. We are having some friends over. Pretty sure the Bramfords will be there. I'll even put in a good word with her old man."

"Why would I need you to put in a word with Mr Bramford?"

"A blind man can see you are sweet on his daughter. You will need all the support you can get. You're not their type. But I have learnt that a business network, is as good as a social reputation around here,"

Flynn sat looking at the envelope sitting on the desk for a while. How many other blind men could see he was totally smitten with the beautiful Miss Bramford? Eventually he cleared his throat, stood up and picked up the paperwork. "I will take the contract and look it over Mr Lincoln. I will give it my full consideration. I'll give you your response by New Year's Eve. But unfortunately, I will not be able to accept your dinner invitation. I have another engagement. Perhaps another time. You have given me a lot to think about."

* * *

Joy stared at him defiantly. "Why not?"

"No. No. If I am ever going to be engaged to you Joy, it will not be done by creating a public spectacle that is enough to make a camel blush."

"But Flynn, it worked perfectly. Mr Lincoln has done nothing to hinder their plans now. He wouldn't be game. The shame would be horrifying."

"I agree. The shame is horrifying. And we won't be following suit."

"Then we are doomed to live apart. I will be forced to marry some dreadful old man, enslaved to a marriage arranged by my mother. My life is ruined!"

"Rubbish. Your father would never see that happen."

Joy rolled her eyes. "Well, at least Father has agreed to be your business partner. That will at least give me the appropriate license to work with you. I can paint or even design interiors while you are away."

"Joy, would you to consider managing some of the projects, just like you did with your mother's renovation? I will be back in town quite often, between receiving new orders from Mr Lincoln and checking existing ones are on track. I know ramping up the timber crew will take some time to ensure it runs smoothly. But in the end, I know your mother will recognise that, you and me... we make, not just good business partners... but good partners."

"I think the main problem is that you refuse to wear a top-hat, and you don't have any friends with a Potts Point address."

He laughed at her. "I *do* have a friend from the Potts Point neighbourhood. I happen to remember a situation, where a wise woman once told Mr Lincoln that it was the calibre of our work that should be judged, not our friends, nor our attire... and I would add... our address."

"Fair enough. We do it your way."

They were interrupted by Dotty who found them strolling around the garden. "Mrs Bramford would have you join the family for dinner Mr Galloway... as Mr Bramford's business partner, to celebrate the arrangement."

As Dotty turned on her heel and left, she could not help but mutter to the trees, loud enough for them both to hear: "Since Mrs Bramford has asked them to wear formal black, no doubt the celebration she speaks of... will be their wake."

Joy stared at Dotty's retreating figure and burst out laughing. "Oh my! If I didn't hold Dotty with the same affection as my aunt, I would tremble to be in business with my family. You are a brave man Mr Galloway."

"Brave?" he squeezed her hand. "Brave is not what I would call it. I am inclined to consider my involvement more reckless than the feared folly of Freddie Rilston. It seems I have a compulsion to put my life on the line, in some hope this arrangement will commend myself to your mother."

"Well then, let's get ready for our wake. It is New Year's Eve after all. Our tradition is that we have an early quiet family dinner, and then Mother flits off for a party to see the New Year in. I will lend you one off father's shirts and a dinner jacket, and I will put on something sober as well."

* * *

Flynn waited for Mr Bramford to pull out his wife's dining chair and then followed suit by holding Joy's chair. She sat with a glorious smile and Flynn joined in with the family banter. They toasted the year that was, and the year to come. They talked about their highlights, and fortunately for Flynn, the impression their renovations had made during their Race Week party was still high on Mrs Bramford's list. As Bennet directed that dessert be served, the conversation turned to darker topics: Louisa's engagement had eclipsed all other events recently. It was all anyone was currently talking about. Competition was not something Florence did easily, and she sighed heavily. "I am absolutely heartbroken for Eliza. It was a shameless affair. It

111

is common knowledge that Mr Lincoln was not even asked about the engagement. Such brazen rudeness! No doubt the girl is already pregnant."

"Mother! How can you say that? Louisa is my best friend."

"I'm not saying it to be controversial Joy dear. It is just an observation of the facts."

"You have no facts. She is not pregnant."

Mr Bramford swirled his glass. "Florence, my dear, I do agree. To have a suitor ask one's parents to be included in young couples' plans is common courtesy. The trend is making that courtesy less and less common. It is the measure of a man, although many people say it is very old-fashioned."

Flynn studied his slice of ice-box cake, topped with caramelised apple pieces, presented with a generous dollop of sweetened whipped cream on the side. But he couldn't bring himself to eat.

Mr Bramford casually rotated his dessert bowl and considered his favourite treat with anticipation. "So, when my business partner takes the time to ask if he can take my daughter on a date, I am inclined to be agreeable. It forestalls the mess that the Lincolns are now faced with."

Mrs Bramford froze. She stared at Flynn, who did look very striking in Mr Bramford's dinner-jacket. She had chosen the style after all. Florence turned back to her husband. "Are you saying they want to get engaged?" she said, swallowing hard on her drink.

"We have discussed it," he said calmly, as he tasted the custard-cream layer on his cake. He took a sip of his wine. "In my mind, it is probably sensible for them to go on a date first. We don't want to rush these things. And we need to give the Lincolns all the space they need to extract the fine press they can achieve from a wedding."

Mrs Bramford's eye lashes flickered. "Actually..." She stared back at Joy. "Do you really want to get engaged?"

Joy gagged on the cream in her mouth, and it smeared over her lipstick, and she dabbed her lips with her serviette. "Of course. But..."

"Well, I see no point in delaying these matters. Particularly now that Flynn has a suitable business partnership. It is appropriate that when you are working so closely together that you be engaged. It could create such a scandal working together without a formal attachment. Surely, it is not an understatement that our little circle has suffered enough controversy over this other matter."

Flynn turned his eyes with wonder and looked at Joy, who was staring at her mother and shaking her head in bewilderment. Florence just rolled her eyes and helped herself to her drink. "Don't give me that look Joy dear. I know well enough that if young people are thwarted in their designs on love that they will find an any other way to be together... improper or not, doesn't seem to matter now-a-days. I've seen the way you look at each other. I am not blind. You couldn't keep your hands off each other at the Christmas party. Since he's spoken with your father there is no need to delay. Be engaged. And then this time next year... or the following May would be better... we can have the most beautiful autumn wedding. We can announce your engagement now and then the date will be reserved. Nothing rushed and very seemly." Then, as if she wanted to add weight to her proposal, she reached over to her husband and took his hand. "And after all James, it is all very fitting that Flynn devotes some time to getting the business off the ground. We do need to protect our investment."

James Bramford nodded sagely and scraped the bottom of his bowl. "I defer to your wisdom, my beautiful wife. Unless the two admirers have some objection to your suggestion... I can't say I have any concerns." He looked at them expectantly, and they both stayed silent. "Well then, that is settled. I think I will have a celebratory second helping of this cinnamon apple ice-box cake. This custard is really quite extraordinary."

* * *

20

Flynn flicked a seedpod into the garden bed as they strolled around the garden under the light of the moon. "Isn't a proposal supposed to be a romantic and surprising moment? I feel robbed of the opportunity to give you that."

"Well, it was better than saying, '*I jes bin thinkin'... let's get hitched in a double harness.*' Besides, I did have a wonderful moment. It was when I realised that Mother wasn't going to fight us on this. I don't think you realise how much of a miracle it is that she has decided to actually advocate for us."

"Happy New Year, Joy. However, it came about... that was the best way to close one Year and open another."

They kissed as she murmured, "Happy New Year. I still can't believe it. I am in a beautiful dream again. I feel that at any moment I am going to wake up and it will have all been an illusion again."

Flynn playfully tapped her arm. "I'm real. You are real. This is real. More real than anything I have ever experienced. We can't imagine us never being like we are now... this is our happily ever after."

They resumed strolling around the garden. He stopped and turned to her, sober and serious. "Joy, come with me to Lenwick. Let me show you where I grew up."

"Oh... you are not from Woolloomooloo? Where's Lenwick? I've never heard of it."

"In the Bush... out West a bit."

"The Bush?" she said sceptically.

"Come and see it for yourself. Bring your painting things... I am sure you will find something to inspire you. You like painting in your garden, so I know you are going to love Lenwick."

* * *

From the moment Joy opened the car door and stepped out into the streets of Lenwick, it felt like someone had pulled back the curtains and the sun was streaming in on her. Every sense in her body was roused from sleep. This felt alive.

"Joy, this is Mrs Trimboli. Her boarding house is a better place to stay than the pub. And her mulberry pie is better than any menu Potts Point could ever conjure up." Mrs Trimboli was a small woman with a big heart. Her Italian features made her smile spread all the way across her face, framed by her dark hair streaked with grey.

"Welcome *mia cara*. It is lovely to have you stay with us. Come. I will show you to your room." As she walked through the rambling old house with wide windows and a back verandah, Joy stepped into another world. Every corner was cluttered with nick-knacks that spoke of her hostess' deep religious devotion and the walls painted rich dark red seemed to run like blood through the entire house.

When they walked down the street, the townswomen stopped to stare at Joy's fancy clothes, with her matching fancy hat, whispering behind their gloved hands about who it was that had brought Flynn Galloway home. The couple wandered around the shops in the main street. There was the seamstress, Jane Townsend, who sold haberdashery and fabrics. Jane timidly shared what a pleasure it was to meet someone with an appreciation for fashionable styles. Jane made up clothes for just about everyone in town. Mostly, in a farming community, that meant sewing work clothes. The

Postmaster General handed Flynn a pile of envelopes and quizzed him about what he wanted done with his accumulated mail. The hardware store reeked of fertilizer and hay which Joy found disconcerting. There was a jewellery store which would order in any sort of speciality items. Mr Bollinger said this was the personal touch of their family business. Joy smiled when they completed the tour of the whole business centre in twenty-six minutes. Not at all like the big department stores and boutiques in Sydney. Yet she found it appealing... and personal. Quaint.

Then Flynn took her for a drive out of town. He turned down a rough track, opened a series of gates, and stopped by the creek. Bottle brush trees were over hanging the bank, their red bristles flowers brushing the surface of the water which ran clear over rocks embedded in coarse river-sand.

He pulled a basket from the boot of the car. "Mrs Trimboli make this up for us." He laid out the blanket and set out the treats made especially for them. They settled down watching the water ripple with sunlight.

Joy was amazed. "Mulberry pie! Oh, this is delicious! You may be surprised, but with all of mother's fancy caterers, I have never tasted Mulberry pie before. It is now officially my favourite."

"See, look at us... a down-and-out kid from Woolloomooloo and fancy Sunshine Sally from Potts Point."

"You were always determined to rewrite that story. You are a romantic Mr Flynn Galloway. What a pocket of paradise you have here, hidden away from the world! You are right – I am inspired. This is so beautiful. I wish I had brought my easel with me. I could paint here forever."

Relief infused Flynn's eyes as he passed her another piece of mulberry pie. "Well, we can come back tomorrow. You can paint here... or can choose some of the quieter waterholes further down. There are some really good yabby spots. Then while you create magic on your cavasses, I can catch up on some jobs that need to be done around here."

Joy gasped suspiciously. "There are *jobs* to be done. What does that mean?" He shrugged and Joy stared at him hard. "You own this property?"

"Yes. I do."

"Flynn Galloway, why are you living in the city when you have a farm of your own which you obviously love?"

"This little piece of land was bought by my grandfather. It was his retirement plan. But the cottage burnt down soon after he bought it. He couldn't afford to rebuild so he did virtually nothing with it but run a few head of cattle. It still has a few out-buildings left... which all need a lot of work. I camp in one of the sheds when I come here."

"Why would you leave this? It is beautiful."

"Simple enough. The block is too small to make a real go of it as a farm. I moved to the city because there are more opportunities there. There is not enough construction work in Lenwick. The Trimboli family has the building-business sown up in this area. They took me on as an apprentice, but you know family businesses... there is no future unless you are part of the clan. I had the option to stay on as one of their crew, but for me to get ahead, I needed to leave."

"I admire your courage to step out. For me it is not so easy."

"What about your artwork? Every piece you paint is you putting yourself out there."

"Oh, come on. I know I am oppressed by my mother's idea of who I should be. She considers that art is only valuable as an investment if the artist is well known. Father stubbornly insisted I go to art school... even though very few serious art students are women. Mother still refuses to talk about it. It was so humiliating for her."

"But you have such a beautiful studio…"

"That was built as a potting shed for the Solarium. Father converted it when I was showing some aptitude, and he willingly retreated to the back corner of the Solarium with his potting table. My studio is perfect… but I feel Mother resents her original concept was sacrificed to give me the space. She tolerates my art as an amusing hobby, but a true woman must apply herself to social responsibilities."

"Ah… that is a significant point on which I agree with your father. It is our responsibility to forge our way into those places where we can truly be who we are and do what we love. No knight in shining armour required."

"Flynn… I need to tell you something. I don't think I want to work on the design side of the business with you."

"But haven't we proven we work so well together? Majestic and grand even."

"I've thought about it a lot… but just because I can, doesn't mean I have to. I want a chance to focus on my art. That is what I love." Joy felt Lenwick was giving her permission to be brave. She felt freer here. More like herself.

"Well, it is a bit inconvenient that you are actually taking my advice. I have been thinking it might be too much, to do both. The timber business is firing up, more than I could have anticipated."

"Has going to the city been worth it? Everything I see around me is so different to that…"

"Sure. I went there for work… and I have more work than I can probably handle now. And I have met you."

"You are avoiding my point Flynn. What about this? How can you just pretend that you don't have access to this. It is amazing."

"I think about it. A lot. I have this idea that perhaps I could take a leaf out of Pa's book... run a few cattle, come back here every so often to refresh the country-in-me. You know, your parents' garden is one of the only places where I get that same feeling as I have here. I've always known the city isn't really me... even with all its prospects. Perhaps that is why Lincoln's offer wasn't too hard to pursue. Now I have a legitimate reason to go scrub. And no one bats an eyelid."

* * *

"My Girl...? Do you have a moment?"

"Of course, Daddy." She put down her paintbrush and swiped a stray hair from her face, smearing a little paint on her brow that furrowed with concern. "What is troubling you?" Her Father rarely came to her studio. He considered it her creative space... private. Sacred almost.

"Trouble? I don't know the meaning of the word. I just wanted to float an idea by you." He pulled up a chair and sat down. He considered the canvas she was working on. It was of an idyllic creek, light dancing on the water, the sway of the breeze, creating the movement of dance among the leaves of the trees. He could almost see them sway. He never thought his Joy had been such a fan of dance until recently. It was leaking out in all sorts of ways. He liked that.

"I wondered if you really wanted to wait so long to be married. It seems you are marking time, to accommodate this artificial timeline that is not at all what your heart really wants. Why should you wait?"

Joy rubbed her nose, smearing more cardamon red across her bridge, her frown deepening. "Daddy? Wasn't this your idea?"

He raised his brow... and thoughtfully rocking his head as he looked at the ceiling. The way he was staring at it, he could well have been gazing at the Sistine chapel's masterpiece. "Well... to go from a long engagement to more reasonable timeframes, is sometimes a bit of a leap. These matters need to be managed in stages."

Joy smiled and noticed he didn't mention the massive leap of morphing a disqualified suitor to eligible status. That was a monumental transformation, grub to butterfly. "I was happy enough to wait, but you are right Daddy. I really would rather not."

"Well then, talk to your man Flynn, and if he is agreeable... let's get you married."

* * *

"So how long do we have to wait? How long do you need?" Joy was disappointed that Flynn was hedging.

Flynn rubbed the back of his neck. "I don't know. Twelve months. Maybe less... ten?"

"That long? Why? I thought you would jump at this."

"Well... to be honest I wanted to build you a house as a wedding present. Your design... on the farm in Lenwick. An art studio that has a front verandah looking towards the creek... wide windows looking out over the paddocks."

"Are you suggesting we move to the country?"

"Well... I wasn't proposing we live out there as such. But if we had a cottage there, it would be a place to go to refresh and to paint... sort of like a rural retreat."

"Oh. A retreat in the country. Hmm. Well, that has the right sense of privilege. Because if you even suggested we were planning to relocate to the boondocks, our engagement would quickly become a disengagement. You must *never* mention moving there."

"I understand you want to live close to your parents. But Joy... building is something I do. I want to do this for you. It has been my dream to build a proper place out there on Pa's block for a long time."

"How about I put together some ideas for a small painting studio. A retreat, like you said. It will give you somewhere to stay when you go there, and sometimes I can go with you. I will certainly not be camping in a shed with the snakes."

Flynn swallowed hard and nodded. He realised then, that he had actually hoped Lenwick would become his homebase. Home he could share with his wife and family. Not just a holiday place.

"And you need months to have this all done?"

"I'll only get a chance to go out there in between my other jobs. If it is just a small studio... easy." He smiled. "That has margins."

"Well then, I had better get you those designs." She reached up and kissed his cheek. "I am so looking forward to marrying you Mr Galloway... in the Spring. Father has managed to cut Mother's original timeframe in half. I like the idea of a Spring wedding... with lots of flowers."

* * *

Mr Bramford looked across the breakfast table as he buttered his toast where Joy was luxuriating in her morning coffee, scratching some ideas for wedding flowers on the pad beside her. Mr Bramford was still in his robe and there was a drawn look across this face. He looked at her sketches. "Spring is a wonderful time. So full of life. I do know how much you love flowers my girl. What a beautiful time to be married. I imagine there will be so much to organise with the shortened timeline. I trust you are getting it sorted. I know how your mother loves her lists..."

The idea of bringing forward the wedding to Spring had Mrs Bramford in a flurry. She bustled into the dining room staring at the book in her hand. She put it on the table and turned some pages as she poured her cup of tea. It overflowed into the saucer. Florence shook her head distractedly and put down the teapot. She drained the contents of the spilt saucer into a spare cup. "You know James, even if the church is available, hiring a venue is going to be difficult with this new timeframe. Booking an appropriate venue is not easy. I really think the whole thing needs to be reconsidered. This does not give us enough time."

"Really my dear? You have exclusive use of the most spectacular garden in the city. We have a newly renovated room that is very familiar with generous gatherings. In this matter you have complete control. You can choose your time. You are not reliant on accommodating anyone else's calendar, timetable, or function."

"Holding a wedding reception at home is a little provincial. It was not at all what I had in mind."

"I hardly call your exclusive Race Week functions provincial, my dear. You have been boldly flaunting the rules for years... with rave reviews, I might add. I think we Bramfords are the kind of people who make the rules, rather than being beholden to them."

"Hmm. True. We could have it here. Spring weather is quite mild. The garden looks amazing. We could even set up the tables outside. With the right planning, it could really attract some social chatter..."

Joy lifted up her eyes from her pad she was sketching on. "Oh, mother that is perfect! Flynn loves our garden."

Mr Bramford looked affectionately at his daughter. "And I think there is something special about the idea that you and Flynn were working together, renovating your own reception venue without even knowing. I suspect Flynn would be surprised by that."

Joy chuckled at that idea. So, like her father to notice something like that. And she wondered again at her father's mystical powers of being able to realign things according to his preference.

Mrs Bramford blinked, as if the mention of Flynn was completely unnecessary given the importance of the occasion. Then she smiled affectionately. "Oh James... you old romantic. You do love these little details. Remember how I helped you with those pots in your old gardening shed? And then you sent those same orchids to the florist, to have them put into my wedding bouquet... and I didn't even know they were the flowers we grew together."

"Yes... just like that." Mr Bramford smiled indulgently. What he remembered was Florence had restlessly visited his shed a couple of afternoons; gardening was not at all interesting for her.

"Of course we can make that work. Joy dear, your father is right: I can organise a Race Week party with my eyes closed. Having your wedding reception here is no different."

* * *

"Flynn... don't look just yet. I have the concept plans for our Lenwick Retreat like you asked and I want you to scan your builder's eyes over them."

His heart sank every time she used that word. Retreat. Joy had latched onto the term like a limpet. He duly complied to her request and closed his eyes. He heard the rustle of paper.

"Okay... now. Open your eyes. What do you think?"

Flynn stared for a full two minutes at the diagram and sketches before he said anything. Finally, he spoke. "This is your idea of a Retreat?"

She nodded.

"This is a full-sized house where I come from."

"Well, you suggested the wrap-around verandah, and a studio room full of windows for natural light. We will need a sitting room, and I have gone for the convenience of an inside kitchen, near the dining room. Of course, aside from the main bedroom, we need a couple of guest rooms, in case visitors come with us on our excursions."

"Hmm. That is some retreat."

"I have a different version for you to look at." She pulled out another sheet and placed it on top. It only had one bedroom, a very small living space doubling as the artist studio, with a small front porch. "Perhaps this is more like the retreat you had in mind."

He held up his plans to the house. "So, if *this* is your retreat, what is that other plan?"

She looked deep into his gaze. "Can I be honest?"

"Please..."

"I can't show this to my parents, they would be suspicious of our intentions immediately. The cottage drawing is just a decoy. Build me this house Flynn, so I can live there with you. We can have a cow chewing its cud, and a horse with a foal. Perhaps even a friendly pig that will wallow in its own waterhole with a duck or two... *This* is the home I want you to build for us."

He looked at her curiously. A broad smile melted over his face. "*Home?* In Lenwick? Oh Joy! That is wonderful! You will love it there, I know!" He swung her into his arms and kissed her hard.

She laughed softly as she came up for air. "Of course. I could instantly see that your heart is there. I will be the type of wife who jealously wants to be where her husband's heart is."

"Hmm. You know... don't pitch that decoy plan to your parents. If they see the plans, I want them to see the real ones. I want to be honest with them. I don't want to start our marriage with the charade of telling a more palatable version just to keep them comfortable."

"But Flynn, what if they call the whole thing off? They are not going to be happy about me moving out there. They will think it is too far away."

"That might be a good thing..." he said with a twinkle.

"I don't want this beautiful dream to be ambushed before it gets off the ground."

"Joy... I think you can give them both more credit. And practically, if we set up in Lenwick, it gives me a base from which I can work the more remote forests. That is good for business."

"Wild frontier man. I am liking this man from Woolloomooloo more and more."

He reached out and encircled his arm around her waist. "You are my Joy. If it comes down to it, you know I will live anywhere with you... as long as it's you."

* * *

22

"Florence, my dear, how goes your preparations for the wedding? Is there anything you require from me?" Mr Bramford sat by his wife overlooking the garden, her planner attached firmly to her hand.

"Oh, James you are sweet, but there is little you could do." She flicked open her notebook and turned the pages. "You have given me the names of those you want included in the invitations. I have that list; Joy's dress is being finished; the attending maids are ready to go to the seamstress... so most of the details are sorted."

"A Spring wedding... that is indeed special. It will be quite the occasion." Mr Bramford said it tentatively with a whole lot of doubt in his voice.

Florence stared at her husband in disbelief. "You bring the time forward, and now you have misgivings! You can't say that and not elaborate. What do you mean James?"

"I mean what I said. A Spring wedding is traditionally romantic and should be very special."

"No. No. You say that with the loudest "*I am not sure*" I have ever heard in my life. What is the problem?"

"No problem, of *that* I am sure. Or... perhaps you are right. I do have one reservation... just a small matter..." He drank his tea calmly and looked over the garden.

She gulped her tea and stared at him hard. "Well?"

"My dear, please be assured that I trust your abilities impeccably. It is just that I was thinking... Joy loves all sorts of flowers, but her favourite flower of all, are Chrysanthemums. I can't imagine her getting married without her favourite flowers."

"So? We include Chrysanthemums. That's not a problem."

"We can't include them, when they flower in Autumn. Traditionally they are the flowers of Mother's Day: May... not September."

"Are you suggesting we go back to the original plan, and have the wedding next year in Autumn?"

"Oh no, pushing it out again would be too disappointing for a couple who are so in love. No, I don't think that would work."

"Hmm. Well then..." she said silently with a deep frown on her brow for a while. "James, this may seem shocking... but what about this Mother's Day. There will be plenty of Chrysanthemums around then."

"Florence, that is a perfect solution! How special for you to have your daughter married on Mother's Day. But what about your arrangements? Will it be too soon?"

"Oh grief no. I've told you it is all nearly organised. It simply means I send the invitations out immediately. Where I had planned spring flowers, we'll use Chrysanthemums instead. Yes, this is entirely doable. We just need to confirm the church, and since we are having the reception here anyway, we have the ability to be completely flexible. The time of Chrysanthemums makes sense."

"You, my dear, are a wonderful Mother. I am very proud of you."

"James, that is kind. I know I have never been a nurturing sort of parent, but this is something that I can do for her. Yes, this I can do." And she rushed off to check the availability of the church and to start writing out the invitations.

* * *

Mr Bramford stirred, sat up straight and dangled his thin legs over the side of the daybed. His trousers sagged, too big for his frame. "My Joy?"

"Yes Daddy? Are you okay?"

"Never better. I know your mother is excited about the wedding preparations, and she assures me everything is on track..."

"Yes. It is. And..."

He shrugged. "My Girl, I know this wedding preparation has been a grand production directed by your mother, down to every last detail. And you have been very gracious to give her all the creative license that she wants... even when it is your wedding. You have not challenged any of her choices, and I think that is generous."

"Oh Daddy, I know this means so much to her. I'd be happy enough with a piece of cake and a glass wine on the verandah for our reception. But seriously, I don't mind. And she seems really happy making it special for us."

"There is no doubt that she has fantastic taste. Your wedding day is guaranteed to be a very stylish and elegant affair."

He didn't move though. It was not a long stretch to know Joy had plans for that house in the country that were more than the occasional visit to paint picture of creeks. He would do the same himself. Eventually he picked up the teapot and topped up his cup. "I trust your mother understands that your country project, this studio Flynn is building for you... is a convenience for your artwork... nothing more."

Joy looked at her father. Yes, he knew that she wanted to live there. "I've... umm... alluded to that. But Flynn is not inclined to soften the blow. He says it is not honest."

He shrugged thoughtfully. "That is one way to look at it. Can you do something for me my Joy?" he said into his cup. "Give your mother this kindness too. Just like you have with the wedding preparations. A large country estate, to visit on a whim... it fits her picture of what life is supposed to be like."

"Oh Daddy, you are an old Romantic. I think you are as much as in love with Mother, then when you were first dazzled by her smile."

"Not a truer word was spoken my Joy. We have defied the tabloids and had a good life together. Now show me, what other wonderful art is inspired by this place by the creek. You have painted so many bottle-brush flowers lately, I think your affection for Chrysanthemums is being challenged."

Joy pulled out a thick timber board. It was encrusted with bottlebrush flowers, bordering a thick scrolled script: *Bottlebrush Grove.* "We have named his grandfather's property after the grove of Bottlebrush trees along the creek. "This will hang by the gate, inviting everyone to our new home." Joy smiled and gently added a tint of crimson to the board. She turned to her father. "Daddy, it truly is the most beautiful place on earth. You will love it so much. I can't wait to show you."

"Do you know my dear... I have already seen it through your eyes and your paintbrush. It is indeed a privilege to visit with you."

* * *

23

Joy ran lightly through the house to the Solarium, followed by Flynn carrying their suitcases. Her father's daybed was empty, and his potting bench stood silent. She frowned and made her way back to the living room. "Daddy? We are back! We hung the sign by the gate. It looks fantastic! Everything is so..."

Dottie appeared and blinked hard. "Oh Joy, you are here. Your mother asked that I bring you up as soon as you were home."

"Oh? Is there another problem with my dress? Will it be ready in time?"

"Your mother said to come." Dottie turned brusquely and took the lead up the stairs. Joy followed in a flurry.

"Dottie! What's going on?" she whispered.

Dottie nodded sympathetically and opened the door into the shadowy room. Joy shook her head in disbelief and rushed silently to the bed. "Daddy! Are you okay? What is going on?"

Mr Bramford smiled wanly from his pillow. "Oh Joy, you are here. That is good. Just resting after a hard day at play."

Her mother pushed aside a knee rug and stirred from the depths of a lounge chair by the window. Joy stared at her mother in shock. She could not remember a time, when her mother's hair was not impeccably styled, and her make-up wasn't picture perfect. "It seems Doctor Bertrand has filed your father's papers. He's been given his ticket."

Joy looked between them confused. "Ticket? Where are you going Daddy?"

Mr Bramford looked indifferent and yawned broadly. "She is being dramatic. She refers to that final great train ride. Bertram says it will not be long now before I depart. But I will remind you Florence, I haven't boarded yet. And I don't intend to... just yet."

"Daddy! What on earth are you talking about? This is not the time for riddles!"

Her mother came and stood by his bed. "Joy dear, your father is being more literal than he ever has been. He means what he says."

Joy stared at his sallow cheekbones and gasped in horror. She fiercely grabbed Flynn's hand who silently stood by her side. "What? No! Daddy, you were fine before we left to go to Lenwick! You can't be like this now. It's impossible!"

"My Joy... it is what it is...". Then, as if the weight of the conversation was too much, he dozed off.

The silence was cold for a long time, interspersed with his difficult breathing. Her mother abruptly stood up, roughly brushing at her eyes. "He must rest. He's had some pain medication," she said tersely. She stared at Flynn severely. "You must leave. The wedding is cancelled. This is a time for family. It was a mistake from the beginning. Get out! And leave us to our sorrow."

Flynn stared around the room; at Joy sobbing by her father's pillow; her mother standing stiff and angular. Mr Bramford's eyes were closed, and Bennet gently directed him by the shoulder from the room. He stood at the front door in shock as Bennet handed him his hat. "Bennet, when they say cancelled... surely what they actually mean is postponed?"

"I suspect that since everything in the Bramford house has been turned upside down, that you best work on the understanding that cancelled is cancelled. Given the severity of the situation, young man, I don't think it would be realistic to assume anything else."

"Doesn't Joy have a say in this? We are still engaged. She has just received the most shocking news. I need to be here with her."

"Can I be frank Sir?"

"Please Bennet, I would really appreciate it."

"Then, let me be clear. Mrs Bramford has said wedding is off. That means you are no longer even betrothed. You are not getting married. I personally think it would be best that you go back to your appalling little humpy in the outback. Let the dust settle and Mr Bramford's ashes cool. This family is living a nightmare, and they don't need you here making distressing claims on their time or fortune."

"Bennet, that accusation is outrageous! I love Joy. I was never after the Bramford fortune."

"Well Sir, you can prove your love and loyalty by leaving respectfully in their time of distress, without making a scene. If you wish to demonstrate the love that you claim, that is the best you can do."

Flynn brushed the hat in his hand in a daze and turned to go. Joy flew down the stairs, into his arms, sobbing so her frame shook.

He held her, soothing her with his murmurs, waiting for her sobs to abate. "Shh now. Just now you need to be here for your father... and your mother. So that is what you will do. Perhaps the doctor has made a mistake, and it will not be like they have said at all."

"Oh! Flynn, no... Don't go. I need you here. You can't leave."

"Joy, it is not that I want to go, but you heard your mother. Being here is just going to cause more conflict and stress... even for you. I don't want you feeling like you have to choose between me and your family."

"I don't want to choose. I want both."

"I know. But for now...you will not only be managing your own feelings, but everyone else's as well. It is best that I leave."

"Oh Flynn... I knew this would happen! I knew! I bet Mother made this whole thing up just to have an excuse to toss you out."

"Shhh... that is very unlikely. When things have settled, send me word. I am going to finish the house, just as we planned and then we will take it from there."

* * *

Mr Bramford sat up in bed and adjusted the covers as a tea tray was positioned. "Florence? Tell me that what Bennet reported is not true. Did you really toss Galloway to the curb and call off the wedding?"

"Of course. My husband is lying here dying, so we cannot possibly have a wedding."

"Why ever not?"

"Because you are *dying* James! I think that is reason enough!"

"That is a matter on which you keep reminding me. I had a bad day or two, but I am not dead yet, and I want to see my daughter married before I do. I want to walk her down the aisle Florence! Don't you dare steal this from me!"

Florence stared in shock at the fire in her husband's eyes and burst into tears. "I can't. I have spent my entire life fussing over the exact shade of tulle. It is a terrible realisation that none of this is terribly important. How can we go ahead knowing what we know?"

He softened and indicated for her to sit by his bed. "Oh come, Florence my dear... hush. When you marry a man forty years your senior, a funeral is always going to be part of the equation."

"Thirty-six. James, this is not funny. I am not ready. It wasn't supposed to happen yet."

"Are any of us ever ready? We try and make ourselves ready, or we do it anyway... unprepared. But I am ready. God has given me a good life, with a wonderful wife, and a beautiful daughter. However, I have asked my good God for one dispensation. Part of my preparation was to see Joy marry the man she loves. That means Flynn, Florence. Please my dear, don't obstruct this. What they have is quite remarkable."

She sighed heavily. "What do you want me to do?"

"Put it back on. Unwind what you did, and make it happen."

"I can't. He has left town. Gone scrub."

"If you hunted him away, then you need to fix it Florence. I don't care how you do it. But next week is my daughter's wedding day. She is getting married, and I am walking her down the aisle. He needs to be here."

"You want to keep to the original date? That's impossible. I've told people."

"I'm running out of options. It needs to be then."

"But...". She shook her head, immobilized in the horror of what was happening. "It's impossible."

"Florence. My entire life I have seen the impossible happen. I assure you, I am staying to see this through. It will either be the spectacular event that you have planned... or a small gathering under the trees with Bennet as the witness. Your choice. Next weekend our daughter is getting married."

"James, I have never seen you this obstinate about anything the entire time we have been married."

"I have never needed to be. But this is too important my dear. I don't want the last memories of my daughter to be with the light squashed out of her eyes. That is not right."

"She is grieving her father. Of course she is sad."

"Then don't make her grieve her husband and dreams as well. It is too much."

"James, I have been thinking... are you sure you want to go to your grave knowing our daughter is marrying some blue-collar chippie? She can do better."

"Florence. We have been through this. Life throws us all sorts of things that are not what we planned or how we think they should be. Regardless of the best installation of lighting plans, there will still be shadows around the fringes of our rooms. Regardless of his occupation, Flynn is honest, and hardworking, and loves her sincerely. That cannot be tagged with a price as if it was a hat."

"But..."

"From those initial meetings I had with Wilkinson about the renovation, when Galloway first arrived in town, I could see he had a different way about him. I decided then that I would see if anything would come of it."

"James... what have you done?"

He shrugged carelessly. "I created an opportunity... that is all. It did cost me to convince Wilkerson to have a family crisis, and Lincoln needed some encouragement to give the Majestic and Grand a makeover. Etcetera, etcetera... but it has been worth every penny to see the light shine in Joy's eyes again."

"You and your opportunities. But James, this is entirely different from going along with all your charades to avoid Race Week. This is our daughter's life."

He looked up at her and grinned. "Charades? You knew?"

"Of course I knew. How could I not? We work together, like synchronised watches."

"My dear, I have a confession. It was just before Race Week that Bertrand told me it would only be by God's grace that I would see six months. That six months is up. I am now officially on borrowed time."

"Back then? How could you withhold such a thing from me? James!"

"And spoil this time with my wife and daughter? Having well-meaning dullards come around to fuss over me, wanting to sing Kum-Ba-Yah by my bedside? I am sorry my dear, but I was not up for that. And don't blame Bertrand – I made him swear on my last will and testament not to spill the beans. I have seen Joy smile again, and paint with the vibrancy that reminds me so much of her mother. After Joseph didn't come home, I feared her broken heart would never be brave enough to love again. It seemed impossible to imagine life could ever be kind to her once more."

"You are serious. You want this wedding to go ahead."

"On my grave..."

"Oh James. That is not funny."

"No. This is my final hurray. I know they are good for each other Florence. If you would just get that picture of two-toned shoes out of your head and look at the man, you would see that too. Why else would I invest in business with him?"

"Very well. I will send Bennet out to that Ludwick place."

"Lenwick."

138

"Ludwick – Lenwick. Tomato – Tomarto. Okay, I will. The wedding will go ahead. *You* had better make sure you are there."

Mr Bramford smiled and nodded. "There. My Florence is back. Thank you, my dear. This means everything to me."

* * *

24

The car chugged to a stop. Bennet stepped out of the car and closed the door. He looked at the dust on his patent leather shoes with a frown and surveyed the frame of the house before him. Flynn put down his saw, spoke to his offsider, stepped over the boards and came towards him. "Didn't expect to see you all the way out here... in the *outback*."

"I have a message from Mrs Bramford, if I may," Bennet said formally.

"Has Joy's father...?"

"No. He is being quite stubborn about that matter. And insistent on another." Bennet reached into his breast pocket and passed an envelope to him. Flynn opened it up and read quietly.

"When is this happening?"

"Tomorrow, at four o'clock in the afternoon. It is the request of the family that you arrive on time."

"Tomorrow? You haven't left any margin." It seemed to be the Bramford way.

"It has taken me three days to get here. Car trouble."

"What happened to 'cancelled is cancelled'."

Bennet shrugged. "The cancellation has been cancelled. I am none too surprised really. I always thought..."

Flynn put up his hand and interrupted. "What does Joy say?"

"Not much. She has been too distraught about her father to say much about anything. But yes, she wants the wedding to proceed."

"That, I actually believe."

"Sir, Mr Bramford is determined that this matter be resolved... before... you know. Can he count on you being present?"

"I will be there... but not for Mr Bramford or his wife. Only for Joy."

"Of course. That is understood." Bennet cleared his throat and yawned broadly. "To avoid being tardy, we are going to have leave immediately, and drive straight through, without any stay overs. It is an appalling state of affairs, but it is the only way we are likely to get back on time."

"Let's hit the road then. I have a wedding to attend!" Flynn opened the driver's side door to the car and jumped in. "Feel free to snooze while I drive." He pressed the ignition starter, and nothing happened. He didn't pause but pulled open the door. "No worries. We take the truck."

* * *

Joy walked around the garden with her father. "You mustn't wear yourself out Daddy. You need to leave something in reserve."

"I'll sit here for a bit, before I make my way back inside." He looked at his daughter. "There are so many things I wish I would have said to you. But my time is done now."

"I wish we could talk forever..."

"I just want you to remember, that when you marry... when you sign that register, Joy you are not just changing your name... but your life. You don't answer to your mother or me anymore, but to Flynn. Make sure your life with Flynn is the way you want it to be... not what you think your mother, or even myself, might want. You do it with him. Will you do that?"

Joy frowned. The speech sounded too serious. The last days had too many tears. Slowly she smiled. "Of course, Daddy. I understand. You give me away and then wash your hands of me."

141

He grinned while he mined wiping his hands and flicking them dry.

"If you had handpicked Flynn yourself, you could not have chosen better. He is a good man, Daddy. He really is."

He nodded affectionately at her joking. "Then I am grateful I didn't have the weight of bearing such responsibility. Arranged marriages are too expensive anyway."

"Ha! And this on-again off-again wedding has not been expensive?" She leant over and kissed his forehead.

He smiled gently. "You have chosen well for yourself, Joy of my heart."

"Be comforted Daddy... you are relinquishing me into very safe hands. I could not be more confident of the future."

* * *

The organ music mumbled away as the guests whispered and fussed. It was scandalous the way the wedding had been cancelled, and then it wasn't. Now the bride had arrived before the groom. She had been sent away to circle the block around the church... three times already. Would she be left at the altar after all the controversy that had already surrounded this wedding?

The organ music swelled in a hopeful crescendo when Bennet appeared, and then faded again as Bennet whispered a message in the ear of the minister and he shook his head. Bennet brushed his cuffs, lifted his chin and sat formally by Mrs Bramford. His suit was crushed and bedraggled as if he had forded causeways and climbed mountains with ropes in the name of executing service. Mrs Bramford's head jolted back with a frown as she caught a sniff of his clothes. "Good grief Bennet, you smell like a stable hand from the racetrack," she whispered in disgust.

"The trip back was dreadful Ma'am. A nightmare. And yes, it included horses. The groom... not a horse-groom you understand... the bridegroom... he is changing his clothes," he whispered.

Flynn came through the vestry door, tugging on his jacket, and adjusting his collar. His chin was rough, and he ran is fingers through his hair as he stood at the front. He nodded to Bennet, who brushed his sleeves again, and took his place beside him, with an air of importance, defying his dishevelled appearance. The minister sighed with relief and finally nodded to the organist. The music burst into the glorious strains of Mendelssohn. The guests rose, lined up along the pews like eggs in a basket. Mr Bramford steadied himself by the door of the church. He extended his arm and glanced at the joy on his daughter's face veiled in a haze of tulle, her beaded headpiece holding her veil close to her forehead.

Mrs Bramford looked down the aisle to where her daughter walked slowly by her husband's side. They paused every few steps so he could catch his breath. Each pew was decorated with fresh chrysanthemums tied with ribbons and tulle creating a delicate floral corridor. Joy's bouquet of chrysanthemums spilled over with a curtain of ribbons as they slowly glided forward to where Flynn stood. Her mother adjusted her gloves as she felt the collective sigh of those around her. She could almost forgive Flynn's bedraggled hair that flopped in his eyes, and his crooked collar, just because the church was so picture perfect.

Mr Bramford handed his greatest treasure over to Flynn's arm. Bennet then supported him to sit by his wife. The wedding service was like every other that had been conducted in that church. Rich or poor, made no bearing on the ceremony. They signed the register, and the newlywed couple was presented to the congregation.

Mrs Bramford's plans then went into motion like a clockwork mouse, wound up by lavish budgets and influential social circles. Flynn was given time for a tidy up so that the newly-wed photographic portraits, against a variety of classic studio backdrops, would not be spoilt. The bridal party of six attendants, which Mrs Bramford insisted were all of Joy's closest friends, crowded into the group photographs. Then they proceeded to their reception at the Bramford home, with exquisite catering, wide garden tables, flowery toasts, and long speeches. Reporters for the social pages interviewed the mother-of-the-bride. Joy danced with Flynn, and with a smile she reminisced of the night he had abandoned her on this very dance floor. He joined her with another memory... the dance lessons that they had together on the glorious stage of the Majestic and Grand. Now they were right here in the Bramford living room, having their bridal dance.

Joy helped her father to the dancefloor, and they waltzed gently for a short time. "You look so lovely my girl," he said affectionately. "Joy of my heart..."

"Thank you, Daddy."

"Don't forget our deal."

"Of course..."

He seemed content then, and they danced silently for a moment longer. "Thank you, my Joy. You have made an old man very happy..." Joy frown thoughtfully as she stepped back and her father took his wife's hand for a slow dance. Not long after that he retired to his room.

* * *

25

Joy laid the bunch of chrysanthemums in her arms on the casket. Dust to dust. She was silent as they watched the men slowly lengthen the straps, lowering it into the ground. Mrs Bramford stood stoically in her veiled black. It seemed impossible to Joy that her father was no longer reading away the hours in his solarium. Mr Bramford, even in his retirement, was a man who was greatly admired and respected in their community. Mourners soberly filed through their home, which only weeks ago hosted their wedding reception.

After the funeral Joy stayed at the house, supporting her mother through the early months of working out the details of what living without her father would look like. Flynn went back to work with his timber crew, and in between, he worked like a crazy man, building their house in Lenwick. Eventually Joy was able to pack up her things, choose her favourite items of furniture from her father's estate and they moved into their house at Bottlebrush Grove. There was only one item of furniture that was brand new: a beautifully handcrafted cedar table, made from a tree Flynn had chosen himself and cut down with his own crosscut saw.

After all the grief and sadness and loss and pain, living at Bottlebrush Grove finally gave Joy's heart a chance to heal. She settled into a routine of making their house a home. Creative projects filled every moment. Each day Joy walked down to her favourite spot by the creek where the bottlebrush leaves gently swept the surface of the water. And she painted and painted and painted. Eventually, Joy noticed she painted less of her sadness, and more of the beauty around her, reflecting a rise of hope and gratitude. It felt like she was sweeping the dust from the corners of her soul, turning on the light to expel the shadows. Every day she could feel her heart mending.

On one of the swings back from the timber camp, Flynn stood at the door of their home and smiled mysteriously. "I have brought you something..."

Joy looked expectantly in his hand, but he extended his empty palms towards her and spread his fingers. "You have to come..."

Joy followed him, and there, tethered to a stake by the shed, was a goat. "Oh Flynn! A nanny-goat! Oh, look at her. She is beautiful!" Joy affectionately stroked her brown coat flecked with white blotches. "I am going to call her... *Spotty*... named with fondness after Dotty of course. I really miss her Billy-Goat gruff ways." She laughed so hard. "Well Mrs Spotty... how do you feel about being the very first member of our Bottlebrush Grove menagerie?"

Oh, how Flynn had missed Joy's laugh. It was good to hear its music again. Adding to their menagerie became the way they marked special days: the anniversary of their first dance or the arrival of Spring, and any other excuse they could devise. Their animals gave them so much to talk about, and laugh about, and be anxious about. Flynn was able to buy his saddle horse and a light harness horse. When he was home, they would go riding together, and sometimes Flynn rode horse out to the camp, instead of driving the truck.

The animals who made their home at Bottlebrush Grove gave Joy so much delight. The pig was a particular favourite. They became her subjects to paint and kept her company while Flynn was away working at the timber camps.

Joy's only sadness was that, as she waited to become a mother... much of her waiting was alone as Flynn continued to work on the business. Her introverted artistic nature meant she spent much of her time in her studio focused seriously on her art. They took trips to Sydney on a regular basis together – one of the neighbours would look after the animals while they were away. During these trips, Joy delivered on commissions she had completed and continued to build her relationship with several city galleries. She would visit her mother while Flynn managed his contracts and attended to business. But it always felt so satisfying to come home.

After one urgent business trip that Flynn made to the city alone, he came inside. The set of his mouth was grim, and his face was ashen. He sat heavily at the table in his work boots with a newspaper in his hand and a pile of letters from the post office. "Joy... have you heard?" She shrugged uncertain and stood up to collect a pot of tea and filled a cup for him. Flynn soberly took her hand. "I have to tell you something," he said as he laid the paper on the table. "Please sit down..."

"What has happened? Is it Mother?"

Flynn swallowed and slowly took her hand. "Sort of... but she's physically okay. The stock market crashed. Really crashed. They are calling it Black Monday... Black Tuesday. I have a letter from your mother's attorney. It's all gone. Your mother will have to sell the estate."

Joy shook her head in disbelief. "Sell! What will Mother do?"

"There might be enough for a modest home; some places are going for a song now... but other than that, everything is gone. This is serious Joy... there is more." He pushed over a letter from Louisa.

"Do you know what it says?" Joy asked as she opened it slowly. He shook his head, while she scanned the pages, tears streaming down her face. She put down the letter and pushed it away gasping. "Oh, this is too much," she cried. "Poor Louisa! Freddie... he... ahh... he fell... and didn't survive his injuries. Oh Flynn... This feels like the war all over again. What will we do?"

"First, I will take you to your mother. I need to follow up with Lincoln about the business. I have to know if that has sunk as well. You can spend some time with Louisa ..."

That visit was an appointment with hell. Everywhere was despair and ruin. They organised to sell Joy's car, and even Flynn's truck had to go when it was clear their contracts were disappearing like a mist. They finally travelled home on the train. It seemed like eons had passed since they sat on the verandah together like this. The last of the spring flush of May was fading, as they looked over the paddocks where their cows grazed quietly, oblivious to the trauma that the world had experienced in a crushing blow. They said nothing for a long time, stunned by the events of those months.

"Well... at least we know what it looks like now. Lincoln seems to think he will survive... but it will be a smaller, less secure arrangement. He's put off a lot of men. It is going to be hard Joy... but I am determined... as far as it depends on me, the men in my crew will not lose their jobs."

Flynn held her... and she felt her breath starting to synchronise to his. "Flynn, there is something I have waited so long to tell you... and I know this is not a good time..."

"Whatever it is... we will work it out..."

"You are going to be a Daddy. I am pregnant... we are expecting a baby."

"What?" He sat straight up.

Joy nodded and sadly smiled at the way this wonderful news no longer seemed so wonderful. "I'm so sorry... not sorry about the baby of course... but the timing... when the world has gone crazy, and everything is upside down. It seems unfair that now is when we are having a baby."

"A baby...". Flynn shook his head, quietly amazed, and gently kissed her forehead. "Do you remember how we talked about Bottlebrush Grove being our retreat from the world? Well that it what it is, now more than ever. This is our haven from the chaos out there. This is for our family... here... where we have a cow and a goat to milk, and chooks to lay eggs, and veges to grow in our garden. This is a good place to raise a family... especially at a time like this."

"So, you are okay with this?"

"Oh Joy... not just okay. This is the best news in the world, at a time when there is no good news left to share. This is a beautiful way to mark a new season in our family. A moment of joy. I couldn't be happier. We are here together. This is exactly what we have always wanted."

He gathered her in his arms... quietly retreating into the still, quiet corners of their life, where everything is ordinary, overlayed with shadows, not perfect... and they allowed the world to fade around them in their embrace and found their joy.

***

The End

Other books by this author

Matt's Boys of Wattle Creek

Maggie & Minotaur

Rose's Diary

Gems of Australia Series:
Sapphires of Hope
Rubies of Ambition
Emerald Dreams

Homes of Healing Series:
The Beachside Cottage
Petra Downs
The Writer's Retreat

Guthrie's Lot Series:
A Spacious Place
A Level Path
The Crying Tree

Pioneers of Grace Series:
Time of Grace
Circle of Grace
Journey of Grace
Mask of Grace
Crucible of Grace
Sculpture of Grace

The Bottlebrush Grove Series
Shadows in the Corners
The Ragged Edges
Scratches across the Surface
Cracked through the Core

Children's Book
The Bush Olympics.

www.ingramcontent.com/pod-product-compliance
Lightning Source LLC
Chambersburg PA
CBHW051705180726
48283CB00004B/1220